Breakaway

the magnussons, book one

NOELLE ADAMS

the magnussons

Breakaway

Runaway

One

FOR AS LONG AS I CAN remember, the Magnussons have been known for their lavish parties.

Thanks to an inherited fortune, they have more money than can ever be spent, and they spare no expense on food and decor and entertainment. Mrs. Magnusson is a kind, outgoing woman who loves to play hostess, so they throw a big party at least once a month.

I attend every one of them and have since I was a kid. The Magnusson twins are three years older than me, but we went to the same school and our parents are friends. My mom and dad aren't hurting for money, but they don't have anywhere close to the fortune the Magnussons possess. They run in the same social circle in Green Valley, North Carolina, however, and so I've always been included in that crowd too.

I'm Lily Carmichael. Twenty-six years old. Only child of brilliant parents. Good at music and word games and daydreaming and being invisible.

Tonight I'm attending the Magnussons' cocktail party. It's a fairly low-key get-together for them, offering drinks and hors d'oeuvres and a lot of small talk to the accompaniment of a string quartet. I've been here since eight, and I'm getting kind of restless.

I want something to happen, and nothing ever does.

At the moment, I'm standing in the corner of a vast living room with six of my friends. People I've known since kindergarten. Green Valley is a small town with an unnaturally high percentage of wealthy people since it was built up around a country club and marina on a large lake. Tonight a group has gathered around Elias Magnusson as it usually does. He's one of the twins. He's got brown hair and blue eyes and perfectly chiseled features—strong nose and chin and high cheekbones. He's wearing a business suit that he's probably been wearing all day.

Around him are two or three members of his entourage. That's what Leo calls his brother's sundry female admirers. I guess I'm probably one of them, although I never think about myself that way.

I don't follow Elias around in hapless adoration.

But I've been in love with him for ten years.

He's responding to something Carter Wilson just said. Carter is a few years older than my group of friends, so I don't know him as well as the others. But like the Magnussons, he's been a fixture in Green Valley life since I was born. He is almost as handsome as Elias—warm and kind and happily married now. I've always really liked him, but I don't know his wife very well since she didn't grow up in Green Valley with the rest of us.

Her name is Ruth, and she must see me look at her. She gives me a wide, genuine smile. I return it since I recognize sincerity when I see it.

I'm still smiling when I turn back to Elias, and for just a moment his eyes land on me. He blinks as if taken by surprise. The corners of his mouth turn up just slightly, which is a dramatic change to his typically cool, stoic expression.

My heart jumps and then begins to gallop. A pressure of excitement rises into my throat. My smile turns a bit trembly, and I don't look away from his eyes.

Maybe, maybe he's really seen me again. At last.

But he turns back to Carter and asks a question.

I wait, almost holding my breath. My heart hammers so hard I'm afraid the others might be able to hear it. But Elias doesn't turn back to me.

He's always been deeply focused, pouring himself into whatever is currently holding his interest, and those interests have never been me. Not since I was eighteen years old and he gave me a single lily.

It was just after my final recital with my piano teacher—the one who'd taught me since I was five years old. It was a big, formal, high-pressure event and the pinnacle of all the intense music training I'd had up to that point. I was nervous and uptight preparing for it, and I happened to run into Elias the day before since he and his brother were back in town from college for their summer break. He asked me what I was up to, and I told him about the recital. For the first time, he seemed to really be listening to me. Seeing me. He said something casual about being showered with red roses afterward, and braver than normal, I told him that would be nice but I'd always dreamed about getting a lily instead. A single perfect calla lily to match my name. I've never been a person who opens up easily, but that afternoon I told Elias that the simple gesture would mean more to me than fountains of roses since it would mean someone really knew and understood me.

The following evening, after I went backstage after performing at the recital, there was a single perfect white lily lying on my black jacket.

There wasn't any note, but I knew it was from Elias. I'd never told another soul about dreaming of that particular gesture.

I'd always had a girlish crush on Elias, but that moment turned it into a love I've never been able to shake despite never getting any further encouragement from him. He's never spoken of it, and neither have I. And most of the time he barely notices I exist, so I have to assume the lily was a random, kind gesture on his part and not an expression of interest.

Even so, I keep waiting. Wondering if he'll ever really see me again.

Eventually, as I stand around with my friends at the party, I start to feel glum and kind of stupid. I don't want to be the kind of person who hangs around indefinitely, hoping for another crumb of attention, so I murmur my excuses and wander away.

Some people love with absolute devotion, waiting chastely for their beloved and never giving themselves to anyone else. That's not me, probably because I've always suspected my love might be futile, and I never wanted to live my life at the mercy of a man—even one I care about as much as Elias. So I date a lot, most of it casual, although I've had a few more serious relationships. I'm always trying to find another man who I can feel about the way I do Elias, but so far it's never happened.

I'm not a silly dreamer. I'm not putting my entire life on hold for Elias. But it still feels like I'm in stasis because I can't seem to break away from the experience of true connection I had at eighteen years old.

I'm greeted as I walk around by a lot of people. They're familiar to me. The backdrop to my life. Some of them I like, and some of them I don't. But none of them are Elias, and the fact that I still can't shake these feelings gets to me after a few minutes. I need to do better than this. I need to move on.

I need to... break away.

I meander back to a door on the far wall and walk into a room I know to be a study.

Bookshelves line the walls, and there's a small bar near the windows.

I head back to it and pour myself a few swallows of Mr. Magnusson's very fine Scotch.

"That bad, huh?" The familiar voice comes from behind me and surprises me so much I actually jerk, sloshing the liquid in my glass but fortunately not spilling it.

"What's bad?" I turn around to face the man I know I'll find. Leo Magnusson. Elias's identical twin brother. Younger than him by twenty-six minutes.

"Whatever is making you take solace in the good stuff." He nods toward my glass.

"I don't need to take solace." I sound and feel annoyed, which is a normal state of mind around Leo.

He does look exactly like Elias. Same thick brown hair and deep blue eyes and ridiculously handsome features. But Leo's hair always needs cutting, and he clearly didn't bother shaving tonight. He's wearing tailored black trousers and a completely inappropriate shirt for his parents' fancy party. A charcoal-gray Henley.

He's sitting in a big leather wingback chair and was obviously reading the newspaper he's holding.

His parents aren't the only people in Green Valley who still subscribe to the paper copies of local and national newspapers, but Leo is the only person I know who actually reads them.

"You look upset." He puts the paper down and straightens up slightly from his ungainly slouch. "What's going on, Lily?"

"Nothing is going on." I scowl at him since I never try to hide my feelings around him. It wouldn't work even if I tried. "I was feeling crowded, so I came here to get a little quiet."

"Sure you did. And your strained expression has nothing to do with my brother ignoring you as usual." No one can make words sound so dry and cutting as Leo.

I give him another scowl as I take a swallow of Scotch. The taste and feel of it hit hard, momentarily distracting me. When the warmth dissipates, I remember it's my turn to say something. So I mumble, "Shut up."

Predictably, that just makes him laugh. "What? I'm just being a sympathetic friend here." He makes an ironic gesture of surrender. "Any friend would want to know how the love of your life is developing."

I roll my eyes and shake my head. With anyone else, I would have been mortified to admit my hopeless devotion to a man who's only once noticed me, but it's impossible to be embarrassed around Leo.

"So my original question holds merit after all," he drawls. "That bad, huh?"

I have no idea how Leo uncovered my secret love for Elias, but he figured it out a long time ago when I was on a summer break from college. He's teased me about it ever since, but he's never told anyone else.

That's one thing about Leo. He might be pesky and often obnoxious, but he knows how to keep a secret.

"It's not bad. It's fine," I say, sitting down in a chair across from him. I want to finish my drink, and my feet are hurting in my heels.

"Maybe. But fine isn't good." He looks like he's going to say something else, but his sharp blue eyes search my face and whatever he sees there causes him to change his mind. "How's your work going?"

Relieved by the change of subject, I tell him about my position teaching music lessons at Hope House, a local community outreach center. I've been classically trained and even majored in piano at college, but I'm not good enough to have the kind of career my parents hoped for. I'm happy with my job, however. I feel like I'm doing good in the world, and I can still spend my life with music.

Plus I'm used to disappointing my parents.

Another of Leo's good qualities—he does have a few—is that he always seems to really listen to what I say rather than faking the conversation while secretly searching for someone more interesting to talk to. From previous conversations, he remembers the names of all the staff members I work with and even some of my students. He's entirely non-annoying for several minutes as we chat.

When it feels like we're only talking about me, I shift the subject slightly by asking, "What about you? How's the dissertation going?"

The Magnusson fortune was made in shipping more than a hundred years ago and has been passed down and preserved by some wise investing despite the family's lavish spending. Mr. Magnusson's only "job" has been managing the family wealth for as long as I can remember, but his sons both have pursued real careers.

Elias studied business and last year joined a corporate consulting firm established by another local boy, Lance Carlyle. And, to my surprise, Leo has persevered in graduate school for several years. He earned a master's in philosophy, and I thought he'd give it up after that, but he kept going toward a PhD. He's finished all his coursework and is working on his dissertation now.

Of course, he's been more than three years working on his dissertation, and the end is not even in sight.

He gives a shrug at my question. "Not bad. Still plugging."

"How much have you written?"

"Five chapters."

"How many pages is that?"

He gives another expressive shrug. "I don't keep count like that. A lot of the work I'm doing is research, not writing."

"Well, give me a rough estimate of the writing."

"Three hundred pages?"

"Seriously? And that isn't long enough for a dissertation?"

"It's long enough, but I haven't finished yet. I'm not going to stop halfway through and call it done."

My mouth falls open. "Are you only halfway through? After all this time and so many pages?"

His mouth twitches. "Maybe a little more than halfway."

"You've got to finish eventually. Don't they cut you off after so many years?"

"Yes. They will. I still have time though."

I peer at him closely, wishing I could read something other than dry amusement on his handsome features. "Do you want to finish?"

"What kind of question is that?"

"A real one. Do you actually want to finish, or are you just dragging it out to pretend you're doing something?"

"I am doing something. You think a dissertation is easy?"

"No, of course not. That's why I didn't take that route. I didn't mean you're being a slacker. You're just not much on…"

He's frowning now. His shoulders rise and fall as he takes a slow breath. When I don't finish the sentence, he prompts, "I'm not much on what?"

I'm suddenly afraid to finish. For just a moment, I wonder if it's possible for me to hurt his feelings.

I never thought I was capable of that before.

His eyebrows arch up very high. "Lily? Complete your thought."

Because I'm not quite sure what he's feeling, I soften my words more than I normally would have with him. "You've always been great at everything you try, but you're not always one to stick the landing. Remember when you started that chess club at school? You got everyone to sign up and even got us in the competitive league and then just dropped us all before the championship."

"I didn't drop you. Something else came up."

With a snicker, I shake my head at him. I'm relieved that he looks amused now. Sardonic. Like his typical self. "That's what I mean. You're smart and talented and good at a ridiculous number of things. You just don't like to finish. So it's a perfectly valid question to wonder if you're planning to finish your dissertation."

"I am. It's not done yet."

"Okay."

"I'm going to finish. I'm not done yet."

"That's what you just said."

"I'm saying it again because it doesn't look like you believe me."

"What does it matter if I believe you or not?"

For some reason, my heartbeat has revved up. It feels like my blood has gotten moving in my veins too. My cheeks feel warm, and I'm trapped by Leo's challenging gaze.

It's a strange reaction. A ridiculous one. I have no idea what's gotten into me, but I just can't look away.

"It matters," he says, leaning forward in his chair.

"Why?"

He opens his mouth, and I have no idea what he's going to say. He's one of the few people I can say that about. I've got a knack for predicting conversations, mostly because I've known all these people for so long, and when you're on the periphery, you have a lot of opportunity to observe. But Leo always surprises me, and I have a feeling he's going to surprise me again now.

But before he can get another word out, the door to the study opens and Elias comes in.

As always, my attention veers toward him immediately. He's got a long, confident stride. Like he's always on a mission. This evening, his mission is clearly directed toward Leo. "Peter Mayer is looking for you," he tells his brother, evidently unaware that I'm even in the room.

"Why would I care about that?"

"Well, you should care because he keeps telling *me* everything he wants to tell *you*, so get your ass up and talk to him before I send him in here after you."

"I'm talking to Lily at the moment. I'll go find him later."

"Find him now. Lily can go with you." Elias's eyes flicker toward me but return to his brother before I can even process the look.

Leo rolls his eyes and hefts himself to his feet. "Fine."

I stay in my seat, seeing no reason to return to the crowd quite yet.

But Leo has other ideas. He glances back toward me. "You heard Elias. Get your ass up. You can come with me."

"Why would I want to do that?"

"Because if you don't, I'll collect all your least favorite people and send them in here to hang out with you, starting with Mariana Brubaker."

With an indignant huff, I get up. Leo is entirely capable of doing something so petty, and I don't want to get trapped like that.

Elias is already leaving the room, but Leo waits to walk with me. He stuns me by asking in a low murmur, "Haven't you ever considered just giving up on your doomed love and finding someone who actually wants you?"

"I've tried."

"Not very hard. I suspect you enjoy it. It makes you feel special."

"You have got to be out of your mind. Why would anyone want this?" When it looks like Leo might respond with something annoying, I go on. "Anyway, I don't know why I keep hanging on. I think it's because it doesn't feel like I've even had a chance. There was one moment when he saw me for real, but other than that, he's never really noticed I exist. I feel like if he ever really *sees* me again, then maybe…"

Leo sneers. "Or maybe you can find someone who already sees you for real."

"No one does." I'm saying the words calmly, without any self-pity or dramatic exaggeration. But I believe it as deeply and surely as I've ever believed anything.

It feels like I've spent my life in hiding, and even when I want to, I can't seem to break out of the shadows.

Leo looks like he might say something. Something I can't predict or even imagine. But then he shakes his head with another shrug.

I give a chuckle as I say to his back, "Fine. Walk away before we finish the conversation. What did I say? You just can't stick the landing."

As he often does, Leo lets me have the last word.

THE FOLLOWING MONDAY is a long day—with a boring staff meeting at Hope House in addition to my normal lessons and classes. So I'm tired and out of sorts when I finally get home at just after seven in the evening.

I live in a nice one-bedroom apartment with a view of the lake. I do get a salary from Hope House, but it wouldn't be nearly enough to cover the expense of living in this building. My parents bought this place as an investment twenty years ago and never did anything with it. It's small but comfortable, and it feels more like home to me than the large family house closer to town where my parents live.

The first thing I do after kicking off my shoes is go into my bedroom and change clothes. The pants and sweater I've been wearing all day are fairly comfortable, but my primary goal is to get rid of my bra. I'm small but curvy, and my boobs don't appreciate being contained all day. Sighing with relief at my bodily freedom, I pull on a soft oversized sweatshirt and a pair of leggings with some thick, fuzzy pink socks.

In case it isn't evident from my invisibility, I'm not any sort of beauty queen. I'm pretty enough in a quiet, pink-cheeked way. I've got really long light brown hair, too large brown eyes, and an asymmetrical smile. I used to stare into the mirror and try to "fix" it, forcing my lips into an even curve, but my bottom lip simply wouldn't cooperate, and it doesn't really bother me anymore.

I like how I look just fine. My looks aren't the reason no one notices me.

I've been wearing my hair in one long braid—my normal hairstyle since I hate the way ponytails pull at my scalp. I tuck back some of the loose strands that have escaped the braid before I turn away from the mirror and head for the kitchen.

Blessing my past self who had the wisdom to make a large pot of soup over the weekend, I warm myself up a bowl and slice off a chunk of baguette. It's a perfectly satisfying dinner, and I eat it on a stool at the island, scrolling through tweets on my phone to see if anything is happening in the world that I need to know about.

I've only taken a few bites when there's a knock on my front door. It paralyzes me for a few moments. No one ever comes over to visit, and the building doesn't allow door-to-door solicitation.

Who the hell is knocking on my door right now?

"It's me, Lily," a muffled voice comes through the closed door. "Open up."

Leo.

Leo fucking Magnusson is knocking on my door.

It takes another few seconds for me to overcome my shock. Then I get off my stool and swing the door open, still holding my piece of bread in my hand. "What the hell do you want?"

"Very friendly welcome." He grins at me—that obnoxiously amused I-know-better-than-you smile. "Do you greet all your visitors like that?"

"I hardly ever have any visitors, and I never invited you. What do you want?"

"I've got a proposition for you. If you'll be civil enough to let me in, I'll tell you all about it."

I stand and gape at him blankly, and he evidently takes this for acquiescence, stepping toward me until I move out of the entry. He's dressed in old jeans and a button-down shirt I know to be expensive, but he somehow makes it look so relaxed it's almost sloppy.

He's still good-looking, of course. Neither of the Magnusson twins can be anything but handsome.

With a quirk of his lips, he reaches over and raises my chin to close my slightly opened mouth.

I recover from my surprise enough to scowl at him. "What do you want, Leo? You've never paid me a visit before."

"I've never had a proposition like this to offer you before. But first, do you have any more of that soup? It smells great, and I haven't eaten."

I grumble wordlessly, but I'm not the kind of person to let someone go hungry just because he happens to be obnoxious. So I ladle out a bowl for him and heat it up in the microwave. He helps himself to the bread and butter and then studies my refrigerator before he decides on a bottle of imported beer.

"Very nice," he says, smiling as he takes the stool beside me and takes a swallow of the beer.

"It's beer, bread, and butternut squash soup. It's not a gourmet dinner."

"It's better than a gourmet dinner." He eats a spoonful of the soup and gives a pleased hum. "It tastes like you."

My whole body jerks in surprise. "What?"

With a chuckle, he responds, "Nothing rude or raunchy. I mean it tastes warm and real and homelike with just a little spice hiding behind the softness."

I curl up my lip, pretending to be skeptical when I'm actually ridiculously pleased. No one has ever given me a compliment like that before. "So what's your proposition? And I can tell you now, if it's anything like the proposition of me helping you with that zoo fundraiser, you can forget it."

"What do you mean? That was a great time. I'll never forget it."

"That's because you weren't the one bombarded by curious monkeys."

"It wasn't that bad." His mouth is twitching again, a sure sign he's trying to contain amusement.

"Not that bad? One of them kept pulling my hair!"

He gives up his attempt at composure and laughs out loud. "I'll never forget your expression as long as I live. I'm not sure why they were all so fascinated with you."

"So anyway, if it's a proposition anything like that, you can forget it."

"It's not anything like that," he says, containing his hilarity although his blue eyes are still warm and laughing. "It's actually prompted by what we were talking about on Friday. About Elias never noticing you, never seeing you."

17

I grow still. "What does that have to do with anything?"

"Well, I had an idea. For giving you the opportunity to let him see you for real. Then, if he's still not interested, you can finally let him go."

"If this is one of your funny, funny jokes—"

"It's not a joke. It's a real idea. I think it can help us both."

With a sigh, I put down my spoon and peer at him suspiciously. He looks serious enough, but Leo is never serious. "What is it?"

"You know we've got our three-week-long-forced-bonding family vacation thing coming up, right?"

"Don't be snide about it. It's nice that your parents actually want to spend time with you. My parents haven't given a crap about me since they accepted the fact I'll never be a genius or a prodigy." My parents are both brilliant and work as scientific researchers—one for a pharmaceutical company and the other for an aerospace company. When it became clear I couldn't care less about science, they put all their hopes for me in music. And when nothing important came from that, they pretty much gave up on me.

"I know," Leo says in a quieter voice. "I know your parents are shit, and mine are pretty good as far as parents go. But I still don't want to face the vacation alone. I've got to have someone to make sarcastic comments to."

I can't help but giggle at that since it's such a Leo thing to say. "So what's your problem? I thought you were going with Penny."

18

He's been dating gorgeous Penny Hibbert for several months, although they've never been joined at the hip. I've always liked her pretty well, but I never really liked her with Leo. I'm not sure why.

"Yeah, that's not happening. She got a better offer."

"A better offer than a first-class vacation with the Magnussons? There's no way. You dumped her, didn't you?"

He gives a slight shrug. "I didn't dump her. We had irreconcilable differences regarding the nature of the relationship."

"Let me guess. She wanted a serious relationship, and you didn't."

"Something like that."

With an eye roll, I say, "Typical. So what, your proposition is that I go on the vacation with you instead of Penny so you'll have someone to make your sarcastic comments to?" I'm barely surprised. Anyone who knows Leo knows his ideas are never normal or predictable.

"Exactly."

"And what is in it for me?"

"You get a chance for Elias to notice you."

"But I'll be with you! How will that get him to notice me? I want him to notice me as a potential relationship. Not as a relationship for his brother."

"I know that, but you don't get Elias."

"I do too get—"

"No, you don't." Leo sounds almost bad-tempered, which he almost never is. "He needs a challenge. A real challenge. It's the only thing that will get him going. And I'm telling you, if he thinks I've suddenly got my hands on something that he considered his, he's going to notice. He's going to notice you."

Despite the ridiculous nature of this conversation, I'm listening. I'm taking it seriously. Because I do know Elias and have all my life. And Leo is right.

But there are principles at stake here, so I say coolly, "I'm not his."

"I know that. But in his mind, he probably thinks you're there for him if he ever decides he wants you."

I square my shoulders with a huff of indignation.

Leo chuckles. "Hey, it's not *my* mind. I know for damn sure you're not mine. It's in *his* mind. If you want to be pissed, be pissed at him. But the point is that you need to prove to him that you're not just there for his taking. That's where my proposition comes in. Nothing is going to get him to notice you like competition, especially with his brother."

My mind is racing now, thinking through possibilities. "Okay, I see your point. But he's a good guy at heart." When Leo looks like he's going to argue, I talk over him. "You know he is. He puts on that cool front, but he's really not."

"Yes, I know that."

"So he'd never try to steal his brother's girlfriend. He'd never do that. You know he wouldn't."

"No. He wouldn't. But he'll notice you. That's the whole point. So when we break up after a few weeks, then he'll have his chance. You said the other night if he could see you for real, he might fall for you, so you'll have your chance too. Then if it works out, you can have all your dreams come true. And if it doesn't work out, you can move on." He's finished his soup and is scraping the bottom of the bowl. "Perfect plan, isn't it?"

"It's a ludicrous plan." I'm thinking it over though.

"And what exactly is your alternative? Putting your life on hold in the vague hope he'll finally open his fucking eyes and see you?" The sharpness has entered his voice again. The tone that surprises me.

"Ouch." I stare down at my half-eaten soup. "I don't think that's what I'm doing."

"It is what you're doing. Not your whole life—you're doing great at that—but your love life is on hold."

"I date. I've dated—"

"I know, I know," he says with another sneer. "I know all about the revolving door of annoying men you date. But none of them really have a chance because of Elias. Are you really going to waste yourself on a doomed daydream for the rest of your life? I for one am getting sick of it."

I want to snap at him, but I can't. Because part of me knows he's right. I glare at him for good measure, but I'm also vaguely mortified. I'm not a weak person. I'm not a fool. And yet in this one aspect of my life, maybe I've been acting like one.

We can't necessarily control who we love, but we can sure as hell control how we act on it. And I do want this endless yearning to finally end.

Maybe this is the way.

I'll have my chance, and if it doesn't work out, I can finally let it go.

"Well?" Leo prompts after a minute.

"How are you this obnoxious?"

"It's a natural gift. Not everyone has it. You're just lucky I'm generous enough to bless you with this much of myself."

I snort and shake my head. This man is enough to drive a girl crazy.

But I'm going to say yes to his proposition anyway.

I'm going to do it.

This might be my one chance, and I'm going to make something happen at last instead of lurking in corners and waiting for it.

Maybe my dreams might actually come true. For the chance of that, it will be worth putting up with Leo and his obnoxiousness in close quarters for three weeks.

Two

I DON'T HAVE ANYTHING appropriate to wear for a three-week luxury vacation with the Magnussons.

Nothing.

My walk-in closet is hardly empty. I've never been a huge shopper, but I'm twenty-six years old and the same size I was at twenty, so I've collected an adequate wardrobe over the years, including several good designer pieces. But I still can't find anything I want to pack.

Leaving unexpectedly for a three-week trip hasn't been without obstacles. I've had a hell of a time finding people to fill in for my lessons and classes at work, and I haven't had much time to shop.

I pull down my little black dress that's always my go-to in dress-up situations. It can travel all right without wrinkling. But I have no idea what else to bring.

When I come out of the closet with only the dress in my hands, Leo glances up from the small red chair in the corner of my bedroom where he's been slouching and reading his phone. "Expecting that one dress to do some heavy lifting, huh?"

"Obviously it's not the only thing I'm going to bring. But it's hard to pack for three weeks when I don't even know where we're going. Does your mom not give any clues at all?"

"Nope. She never does. But we always spend a week at three different places each. One is always a European city, one some sort of beach destination, and one is always a wild card. Last year we went to Monaco, Hawaii, and a wildlife resort in South Africa."

"Oh my God. She could choose anything. How the hell am I supposed to pack?"

"Bring some beach stuff for sure. And I'd also bring some stuff you can wear in colder weather. And if you need anything else, we can just buy it when we're there. That's what I always do." He's looking particularly relaxed in jeans and an old black sweater. He took off his shoes when he walked into my apartment, so I can see his toes clenching into the carpet in his socks as he stretches out his legs.

It's strange to notice something so small and domestic about Leo. It makes my stomach tighten.

"What?" He arches his dark eyebrows at me.

"Nothing. That makes sense. I'll do the best I can, but I don't want to spend a fortune buying myself a whole new wardrobe just to go through with this wacky plan with you. So I'll probably be wearing the same outfits over and over again."

"That's fine with me. What do I care what you wear? And if you need anything new, I'll buy it for you."

"I'm not going to let you buy my clothes."

24

"Why not?"

"Because. It's weird." I stare at his innocently questioning expression until I see his mouth twitch. "Asshole."

He breaks into a full smile. "Always. But seriously. If you need anything for the trip that's too expensive or too impractical, I can help you out with it. It's only fair since the trip was my idea."

"Well, that's true anyway." I can't help but smile back at him. I'm really not sure how he does it even when he's been annoying. "But I thought you came over this evening to work out our backstory. Not to sit there and make obnoxious comments."

"Can't I do both?"

"I'm sure you can, but we'll get more done if you try to curb the obnoxiousness for a little while."

He straightens up and puts down his phone. "I'll try. So when did you fall in love with me?"

"What?" I gape at him, my cheeks flushing and my mouth falling open.

He chuckles. "Aren't we working out a backstory? Why do you look so horrified?"

I'm a little embarrassed about my reaction, so I turn back toward my suitcase as I reply, "Oh. Right. But in our fake relationship, you're going to be the one who fell for me first."

AN HOUR LATER, I'M packed for the trip, and we've worked out as many details about our pretend dating as we think we'll require. Mostly we just need to be on the same page if anyone asks us personal questions about how we got together so unexpectedly.

It's not hard to do. We've known each other for a really long time. There wouldn't be any of the getting-to-know-each-other that usually takes the longest in a developing love story. We'd just need the spark of attraction to hit us and for one of us to make the move on it.

Our story sounds perfectly natural. Believable. Likely even. I'm not sure if that's a source of relief or discomfort.

"I can take this with me and put it with our luggage so you don't have to haul it down yourself in the morning," Leo says, putting his hand on my large suitcase.

"Oh. That's okay. I can get it."

"I know you can, but why should you?" He gives me an impatient look. "Why make things harder on yourself just because you want to be stubborn."

"I'm not being stubborn. I've got a few more things to add to it."

"So add them now. What's the problem?"

I stand frozen for a moment, trapped by embarrassment and indecision. I'm not a particularly modest person, but I'm also not someone who flaunts her sexuality for the world to see. So under normal circumstances, I'd never even consider what I'm tempted to do just now.

But Leo is looking far too smug. And faintly exasperated.

It's a challenge to me in a way I almost never feel.

"What the hell, Lily?" he demands.

It's his tone that decides it.

With a cool look and not a single word, I step over to my nightstand and open the top drawer. I have a small collection of vibrators, and I pick out a smallish one that's relatively discreet (and not very loud). Then I carry it back to my suitcase, unzip one of the side pockets, and slide it in.

As I zip it up, there's a rush of excitement and nerves filling my head and chest. I do my best not to show it though. No sense in giving Leo the satisfaction.

He hasn't said a word as I've added the last item to my bag. He's standing near me like a statue.

When I finally turn around to face him, I see something hot in his expression.

Hot.

Unfortunately, it makes me feel hot too, and I'm acutely aware of the breadth of his shoulders beneath his thin sweater. The faint bristles on his jaw and down his neck. The way his hair glances against his ears.

With effort, I manage to pull myself together. "No smart-ass comments?"

He clears his throat. It looks to me like he's trying to provide some of his typical banter but can't get anything said.

I shouldn't like the fact that he's reacted like this, but I do.

I really do.

"So now that I've managed to shut you up for a few seconds, you can take my bag with you as you go."

He reaches over to grab the handle of the bag and sets it on its wheels. Then he gives me his quirk of a smile as he starts to leave. "Don't imagine you've shut me up for long."

~

"SO WHAT EXACTLY HAPPENED here?" Elias's face is normally cool and composed, but his eyebrows are lifted just slightly now, conveying the extent of his surprise at the revelation of his twin brother's new girlfriend.

I'm sitting in a small lounge at the airport in Charlotte at almost eight in the morning, and Leo is beside me with his arm slung across the back of my seat. We're flying out on a private jet as soon as his parents arrive.

"We got together," Leo said, sounding bored and slightly impatient, a very typical and convincing tone. "I assume you're not looking for all the dirty details. And there are definitely some dirty ones."

I elbow him and mutter, "Shut up." Only after the words come out do I realize they might not be a good way to convince Elias that we're romantically involved.

Leo turns to give me a heavy-lidded gaze that's somehow both lazy and challenging at the same time.

It annoys me enough to inspire me on what next to say. "Don't give me that look. Our dirty details aren't for public consumption."

He chuckles and leans over until his breath wafts against the skin of my cheek. In a low, decidedly sexy tone, he murmurs, "Can you at least try to pretend not to want to swat at me all the time?"

There's no way Elias heard those words. He probably thinks it's private flirtation.

I shift positions so I can say against his ear, "If you wouldn't act so swattable, I wouldn't feel the need to swat at you."

He chuckles. "Can't help it. It's my natural personality. I can only be what I am." Then, instead of straightening up as I expect, he brushes his lips against mine in a featherlight kiss.

I'm stunned—utterly, completely—at the lightning strike of pleasure the kiss provokes in me. It's like all the nerve endings in my body fire up all at once.

From nothing more than a tame little kiss.

Instead of pulling back and composing myself, I lean forward to chase his mouth as he withdraws, kissing him again, seeking that rush of feeling one more time.

He's evidently surprised by the move. I hear his quick intake of breath before he curves one hand around the back of my head to take control of the kiss.

It's not deep. No tongue is involved. And it only lasts six or seven seconds. But my whole body is hot and pulsing as Leo releases me.

I stare at him for a minute, relieved to see a similar response in his eyes, even as he holds a dry half smile.

Then I remember Elias and glance over to see what he's doing.

He looks surprised. And slightly disturbed.

It's probably a good sign. Evidence that he's noticing me. Seeing me for the first time in years.

I'd be able to enjoy it more if I could get that kiss with Leo out of my head.

THE FIRST STAGE OF THE Magnussons' vacation is Prague. I've never been there before, and I've always wanted to go, so I'm excited when the pilot announces our arrival and I discover where we've been heading all this time.

Traveling with the Magnussons isn't like normal travel. The private plane. The limo waiting at the airport. Even a private customs and immigration window so we don't have to wait in the long line. Mr. and Mrs. Magnusson have always been kind and friendly to me, and now they're even more so. Elias works on his laptop most of the trip, but it doesn't even bother me because Leo and his parents are entertaining enough to make the hours fly by quickly.

Everything goes so well that I've let go of most of my concerns as we check into the gorgeous, five-star hotel.

Until we get to the room that Leo and I will be sharing for the week and discover there's only one bed.

It doesn't appear to faze Leo. He tips the bellman and walks over to look out at the picturesque view of the city through the glass door that leads to the small balcony. Only when he turns around does he see me standing like a statue and staring at the bed.

"Oh. Sorry about that. I was going with Penny when we made plans."

"Yeah. Of course you were. But what are we going to do?" My heart is hammering—hard and fast and loud.

"Nothing to worry about. I can go down and explain you snore like a bear so we need a room with two beds so I can get a little sleep."

I choke on a quick surge of amusement. "I don't think so. If I snored that bad, you could still hear me from another bed. A more convincing story would be you flail around in your sleep and sometimes clobber me accidentally, so we need two beds for my own protection."

"Nah. My folks and Elias would know that's not true. How about you are a ruthlessly insistent cuddler at night and I can't sleep if I get too hot."

I laugh out loud. I really can't help it. "I'm not a cuddler!"

He's smiling now. And it looks like it's for real. "I have my doubts about that. But seriously, if you're uncomfortable with one bed, I can go ask them to move us. Or I can have them bring in a rollaway or something."

Now that my surprise has worn off and his offer seems so genuine, I've decided the one bed isn't really that big a deal. If we're supposed to be in a relationship, we should share one bed. And it's not like Leo is going to make a move on me without permission.

"I think it's okay. I hadn't thought about it, so I was surprised, but I'm not really uptight about things like this. And I'm definitely not a cuddler. We can share, as long as we each stay on our own sides."

Leo gives a crisp nod. "It's a deal. Believe it or not, I'm not a cuddler either."

FOR YEARS NOW, I'VE had the habit of bringing myself to orgasm with my vibrator every night before bed. I'm not sure when exactly it started. Sometime after college when I was going through a dry spell in dating. I'd feel restless before bed and so got into the routine, and now I do it every single night.

It's never been a big deal. I don't have long, sexy sessions or anything. Just a quick three or four minutes to a satisfying release. Then I'm more relaxed and I can sleep.

It's become such second nature to me that I didn't even think about logistics, but by the time it's bedtime in the room I'm sharing with Leo, I start to realize my problem.

What the hell am I going to do? While I'm not particularly embarrassed about my sexual needs, I'm definitely not going to do it in front of him. And I don't even really want him to know.

The afternoon and evening went fine. We rested some and then went out to walk around the nearby neighborhoods before coming back and getting dressed for a lovely dinner and lingering drinks. Elias has included me in conversations in a way he's never done before, and I haven't been particularly annoyed with Leo. I'm pleased with how the day has gone and ready for a good night's sleep. I'm more tired than usual from the time change, so I think about skipping the vibrator tonight.

But the familiar pulsing between my legs is a warning. My body knows what it normally gets before bed, and it wants what it wants. I'm not going to be able to sleep if I don't have a good orgasm first.

Leo and I are back in the room now. He's sitting in the desk chair, scrolling through something on his phone, and I'm putzing over my suitcase, pretending I'm getting things organized.

What the hell am I going to do?

Obviously, the only place for a masturbation session is in the bathroom, but he might be able to hear the vibrator through the door.

Does that matter?

Should it matter?

I don't know, but something inside me definitely doesn't want him to know what I'm doing.

I finally decide to take a shower. That's a reasonable thing to do before bed, and maybe I can get myself off with my hand and not have to worry about the vibrator.

I gather up my pajamas and toiletries and slip in my vibrator just in case and then ask Leo if he needs to use the bathroom before I go in. He doesn't.

The shower is a good one. Excellent water pressure and very hot water. I pull my hair into a messy bun to keep it out of the spray and let myself enjoy a long, relaxing shower.

I rub my clit until I have a quick little orgasm, but it's not as good as with the vibrator, and so it doesn't feel like enough.

It's ridiculous I'm so worked up about this. Leo isn't going to care what I do. I want to sleep tonight, so I need to do what's necessary.

Besides, I realize with a quick brainstorm, he probably won't be able to hear the vibrator if I keep the shower on.

I'm ridiculously excited when I've come to this conclusion. I don't know if my vibrator is waterproof, and I'm not going to risk it, so I get out and dry off, leaving the shower running.

I prefer to lie down, but there's nowhere in this bathroom to do it, so I stay standing, leaning over to brace myself against the wall with one hand as I turn on the vibrator and press it against my clit with the other.

A moan comes to my lips without warning at the intense feel of the vibrations against my sensitive flesh.

It's not loud, but it sounds sensual to my own ears. I plan to make this session as quick as possible, but I keep thinking of Leo in the room on the other side of the door. Idly reading his phone. I remember our kiss earlier and how hot and needy it made me feel.

Then I catch a glimpse of myself in the large bathroom mirror. I'm bent at the waist with one hand flattened on the wall. My breasts are swaying, and they look particularly lush and sexy from this angle. My hair is falling down out of the clip and all over my face.

I feel like a sexy stranger, and my body responds to the stimulus. I moan again as climax mounts, biting my bottom lip to stifle the sound.

The depth of my first orgasm surprises me. My body shakes through it, and my eyes roll back in my head. It's not enough. I need more. So I reposition the vibrator slightly and move my hips like I'm riding it.

The next orgasm is stronger, better. I'm stifling moans as the pleasure throbs through me. Leo is too close to let myself go completely.

But the idea that he might hear makes me even hotter. I'm not sure why since I've never really been like that. For whatever reason, I have to go for a third. I'm panting and shaking and pushing against the wall, and another glimpse of myself in the mirror pushes me over the edge one more time.

I nearly sob with the pleasure of it. The spasms of release that pulse through my body from my center to my fingers and toes. It's so good I kind of want another orgasm, but my clit is too sensitive now, so I turn the vibrator off. The soft hum silences. Every part of me is throbbing deliciously when I finally straighten up.

My cheeks are deep red. My eyes are glinting almost wildly. My hair is a mess, half in the clip and half out. I'm completely naked and kind of like the look of my body.

What would Leo think if he could see me now?

I shake that thought away and turn off the shower at last. I pull on the pajamas I brought—fuzzy blue pants and a matching knit top—and I do my nightly face routine and brush my teeth and go to the bathroom and wash my hands.

Tired and fully relaxed, I open the bathroom door. Leo is still in the same place, reading his phone.

He glances up casually. "That was a long shower."

"Yes. It felt good. You should take one too."

He stands up and stretches his back. "I'm definitely going to take one."

"Okay. I'm going to bed. Take your time. The lights don't bother me when I sleep, so there's no hurry in turning them out."

He mumbles something and goes to where he set his suitcase.

I take a swig of the water bottle next to my side of the bed and crawl under the covers.

I told Leo the truth. Lights have never bothered me when I'm sleeping. Now that I've had three deeply satisfying orgasms, I'm not going to have any trouble going to sleep.

I stretch out under the sheets as Leo heads into the bathroom.

My body is still pulsing from the enjoyment I gave it. I close my eyes and smile.

I hear the shower spray turn on. I wonder what Leo looks like as he's taking off his clothes.

I'm asleep before I mentally remove anything more than his shirt.

Three

THREE MORNINGS LATER, I wake up to find Leo still asleep beside me.

He's usually awake before I am. He gets up early to run—even in the cold and even on vacation. For such a laid-back, relaxed guy, he's remarkably committed to his exercise routine.

But today he's still in bed, and a glance at the clock proves it's not particularly early. He either overslept or he's skipping his run today.

The past few days have been better than I expected. I've actually had a really good time, sightseeing with the Magnussons and hanging out with Leo. I've spoken more with Elias than I ever have in my life, but I'm not as excited about that as I would have expected. Mostly, I just like the feeling of companionship. Fellowship. Family.

Of course, not all the things I've been feeling are familial. Leo is far too attractive for me not to notice when I'm in such close quarters with him. Even in my daydreams, I never experienced this kind of bone-deep lust for Elias. Naturally, I imagined a very good sex life with him, but my dreams were about him romancing me, sweeping me away.

I never needed to claw his clothes off the way I sometimes want to do with Leo.

It's probably just because we're acting like we're in an intimate relationship and he's an undeniably good-looking guy.

He still drives me crazy most of the time. Only I want to kiss him at the same time I want to smack him.

Last night, he and Elias were hanging out at the bar downstairs when I came up to bed. I was having a good time, but the idea of having the hotel room to myself was too tempting. I had a very good time by myself in the bathroom with my vibrator without the pressure of worrying that Leo could hear.

I wonder why he isn't running this morning. Finally finding enough energy to roll over, I reposition myself on my side to face him. His eyes are closed. His face is softer than normal. He desperately needs to shave, and I desperately need to run my hands over his jaw and neck to feel the thick stubble.

It's strange to see him like this. It makes my stomach clench. He's always seemed so sharp and bright—like a dagger glinting in the sun—but he's just a regular man. Human. He's breathing loud enough for me to notice. Slow and steady. He was telling the truth when he said he's not a cuddler. He's always stayed on his own side of the bed at night. He gets hot a lot as he sleeps and sticks one foot out from under the covers, pulling the tightly tucked sheet out of the mattress. His foot is dangling all the way off the bed at the moment.

It makes me smile.

I've needed to pee since I woke up, and the need finally gets too intense. So I carefully climb out of bed, trying not to shake the mattress too much, and I hurry to the bathroom in my bare feet.

After I go, I wash my face and brush my teeth. My hair is a rumpled mess since I always sleep with it loose, and the neck to my pajama top is askew. I don't look gorgeous or sexy, but I don't look terrible either. I kind of like how I look. Relaxed. Natural. I'm not used to that feeling since I spent a good portion of my life wishing my face and body were different than they are.

I smile at my reflection and like how I look even more. I wonder what Leo thinks when he sees me. Then I shrug off the thought.

It doesn't matter. I'm not on this trip for Leo. I'm here to find out if my life's daydreams have any foundation at all.

When I step back into the room, it's still mostly dark. The sun must be starting to rise because there's faint light around the edges of the curtains. I'm walking as quietly as I can when Leo says from the bed, "Why are you tiptoeing like a cartoon burglar?"

I jump and make a soft, shrill sound of surprise. "I was trying not to wake you up. You almost gave me a heart attack!"

He chuckles and shifts position. He's pushed the covers down to his waist. "Sorry. Next time I'll snort and guffaw a few times so you know I'm awake."

"Guffaw?"

"What's wrong with guffaw. It's a good, concrete word." There's a smile in his voice.

I crawl into bed beside him, yanking the covers all the way up to my shoulders. "It's an archaic word. Who uses that word anymore?"

"I do. You just heard me."

With a scowl, I roll back over to my side so I'm facing him. "And I stand by my claim that it's a ridiculous word."

"Wow, you wake up just as argumentative as you are later in the day." His expression is sober as he looks at me, but I can see the smile lurking in his eyes and the corners of his mouth.

It makes me want to smile back, but I resist the impulse. "I'm not an argumentative person. I'm a nice, agreeable person. Ask anyone."

"It wouldn't do me any good to ask anyone else since you're not argumentative with anyone but me."

I think about that for a moment and come to the conclusion that it's true. I'm not sure why or how, but Leo definitely pulls that side out of me. "Huh."

"I'm right, aren't I? When am I going to get gifted with some of your agreeableness?"

"When you refrain from your assholery for a few minutes at a time, then maybe I'll be more agreeable with you."

His mouth twitches irresistibly. "Assholery."

"It's a good, concrete word, and it's a perfect word to describe your attitude. Ask anyone."

"I'm not going to ask anyone else about you or me. I come to my own conclusions."

"And what are your conclusions?" I'm not sure what's gotten into me. I almost sound flirtatious, and one thing everyone knows about me is that I have no idea how to flirt.

He reaches over and pushes some of my messy hair back from my face. The slight touch surprises me. Makes me flush. "My conclusions," he murmurs very softly, "are that you show me a side of yourself that you don't let anyone else see. And if it's my assholery that brings it out, then there's no way in hell I'm going to dial it back."

My mouth parts. My breath hitches. I stare at him, transfixed by the sudden intensity of his deep blue eyes.

For a few seconds, I'm sure he's going to kiss me, and there's nothing in the world I want more than that.

But this is Leo.

Leo.

And he might be acting all soft and warm right now, but that's not who he is most of the time. I'm on this trip to get some closure with Elias. I'm not here to fall hopelessly for another unobtainable Magnusson man.

Leo isn't a closer. He never sticks the landing. He doesn't finish what he starts. He might be having a good time playing around with me, but I'd be the biggest fool in the world to take him seriously.

So I roll my eyes to shift the mood between us. "Typical Leo. So smug you don't think I act like this with anyone else."

"Do you?" His eyebrows pull together, making three little vertical lines between them.

"Maybe I do." I clear my throat since I'm not sure how to smooth out this weird conversation. "Why didn't you get up to run this morning?"

"I was tired," he says with a shrug, flopping back down on his pillow to stare up at the ceiling. "As you know, self-discipline isn't my greatest strength."

"What is your greatest strength?" The question is spoken in a teasing tone, but I really do want to know his answer.

"I'm not sure. You'll have to tell me."

"I'll have to think about it. Now, if you ask me about your most obnoxious qualities, I'll be able to provide you with a comprehensive list."

He laughs low and soft. I really like the sound of it. He makes other people laugh all the time, but I don't hear him laugh that way very often.

It always feels like a victory when I can make him laugh like that.

~

MRS. MAGNUSSON HAS A PLAN for every day of the vacation. I'm convinced she spent the past three months planning out every detail.

The good thing about that is we're never unprepared, we don't waste time trying to figure out what to do, and we don't run into any logistic obstacles. The bad thing is we have to do what's on the list for the day, no matter what we happen to feel like.

I don't actually mind since I'm a fairly organized person by nature, and I don't like to lie around and do nothing in a cool city I'll probably never get to visit again. But we're almost halfway through the first week now. By lunch, after a full morning of museums, Mr. Magnusson is clearly getting tired, and Elias, who would obviously prefer to do his own thing, is trying to play along for the sake of family peace but seems to be champing at the bit. Mrs. Magnusson appears to be more on a mission than ever, so there's not much chance she's going to pick up the signs.

Leo has been his sardonic, laid-back self all day. I can't actually believe he's having the time of his life, walking through one crumbling historical landmark after another, but he hasn't voiced a single complaint. He told me yesterday that he learned a long time ago to just go along for the ride on these family vacations and not push for anything different. He enjoys them more when he isn't wishing for something else, and since his parents are paying, they should get to decide.

I've been doing the same thing, and I figure Elias can rein in any complaints he happens to have. But I hate for poor Mr. Magnusson to spend another afternoon on his feet when he clearly just wants to take a nap.

So I risk a casual suggestion. "I'm excited to see the Strahov, but Leo is kind of a slacker and is looking tired." I give him a playful little nudge with my elbow. He doesn't look particularly tired, but I figure it's better to blame it on him than his father. "Maybe we should split guys and girls for the afternoon. Mrs. Magnusson and I can get everything done we want, and you all can do something less energetic. What do you think?"

"Please, Lily, dear, you need to call me Crystal," Mrs. Magnusson said.

"I'm sorry," I tell her with a little smile. "I'm trying to remember. But what does everyone think of that plan."

Mr. Magnusson's face has broken with relief, and Elias has perked up noticeably. "I think that's a great idea," he says. "Dad and I were talking about checking out that bookstore."

"Fine by me," Leo says, "although I'm not as tired as you think. I'm sure I can summon the energy to join the ladies. I know how much you'll miss me." His eyes are teasing as he tugs a piece of my hair.

I give this comment the eye roll it deserves.

Mrs. Magnusson tsks her tongue. She's an attractive, always perfectly dressed woman in her fifties, and I marvel at how well she can maintain her lipstick throughout the day. "Don't be silly, Leo. You men aren't as necessary as you seem to believe. Lily and I will have a very good time without you."

I giggle at that since I never knew she had any sort of a sense of humor until this week. Leo catches my eye with an unspoken question, and I see immediately what he's asking. He wants to know if I'll be okay by myself with his mother. He'll push to come along this afternoon if I want him to.

Such a little thing, but it fills me with a warm sense of security.

"Yes," I tell him with another light poke with my elbow. "We'll be very happy without you to pester us. You should go to the bookstore too. There might be a comfortable chair you can nap in."

Everyone laughs at that except Leo, but it's impossible to miss the smile in his eyes.

We've been eating lunch at a quaint, quiet café— inside since it's too cold to comfortably eat outside—but everyone is finished now, so we split up and head off in different directions.

I'm a little tired too but not so much that it's a problem keeping up with Mrs. Magnusson—whom I can't think of as Crystal no matter what I do. We head to the Strahov Monastery and Library, and I actually have a pretty good time. She tells me funny stories about the boys as kids, and she asks me about myself, clearly making an effort to get to know me better as a person and not just one of the many young people on the periphery of her sons' lives.

It's almost five when we get back to the hotel, and I immediately spot Elias and Leo hanging out in the lounge area, drinking beer.

"You haven't been drinking all afternoon, have you, boys?" Mrs. Magnusson asks in a tone that makes it sound like her sons are eighteen rather than twenty-nine.

"We needed something to do. You took Lily away from me, and Dad wanted to take a nap. So Elias and I decided to get drunk off our asses."

A quick look at Leo's face proves this isn't anywhere close to true. He's probably just finished the one beer.

Mrs. Magnusson comes to the same conclusion. "Don't be crass, dear. I'm going upstairs to rest before dinner. I'll leave you young people to do whatever it is you do."

I'm laughing as I wave her off and sit down at the table with the guys.

"You want a beer?" Elias asks me.

"She doesn't like beer. White wine?" Leo arches his eyebrows at me as he stands up.

"Yeah. Whatever they have open is fine. Thanks."

As Leo crosses the room to reach the bar, Elias smiles at me. Not warmly. He's always as cool as a crisp autumn breeze. But it seems sincere. "Thanks for going with Mom this afternoon and giving us a break."

I smile back at him, pleased that he recognized my intentions. "It was no problem. I had a good time with her."

"That's good. We've always had a hard time convincing her that she needs to schedule in some downtime. She says that's what the beach week is for."

"So she won't have every day scheduled next week?"

"Probably not. She'll schedule a couple of days but let us lie around on the beach for the rest of them."

"Oh good. Then I can recover."

"Are you having a good time so far?" Elias's eyes are holding mine. They're so much like Leo's—and yet not like his at all.

"Yes. I really am. Better than I was expecting, if you want to know the truth. I wasn't sure what someone else's family vacation would feel like."

"Especially since you and Leo haven't been dating for very long."

"Yeah. I guess. Although I've known him forever, so it's not like we're just starting out."

Elias's eyebrows lift slightly. "So it's serious?"

I shrug. What the hell am I supposed to say to that? "Too early to tell. But it doesn't feel like it's just starting out if that makes sense."

"I guess so." His eyes haven't left my face since we began this conversation. "I never would have pictured you and Leo together."

"Why not?"

"I don't know really. Just that he's always gone for the flashy kind of women."

I snort. "And I'm not."

"No." He's let the word linger in the air when he suddenly straightens up. "I didn't mean that as an insult."

"I know. I didn't take it as one. I'm about as far as possible from being flashy. Kind of invisible really."

"Is that how you feel?" He appears genuinely surprised.

"Yes. All the time. Like I go through life without people really seeing me."

He gives a soft huff of dry amusement and glances away. "I feel that way a lot too."

"You do not!" I'm so shocked I don't guard my words or second-guess whether this is a wise thing to say. "I can't believe you feel that way. You're like the prince of Green Valley."

He curls up his lip and meets my eyes again. "You think that's who I really am? When someone sees me that way, they're not seeing who I really am."

I'm so caught up in the conversation that I don't see Leo returning to the table with my wine. Not until he's sitting down beside me as I finish my response. "I had no idea you felt that way. I had no idea we might have felt alike in that way."

"Alike in what way?" Leo asks, his eyes moving from me to his brother and back again. Almost suspiciously.

I shrug since I'm not sure Elias wants me to repeat what he said.

He confirms it by saying, "Nothing that has anything to do with you."

Leo's face is composed, but beneath it he seems to be hiding a scowl. "If you're bonding with my girlfriend, then I'd kind of like to know about it."

I give him a poke as I take a sip of wine. "Don't be ridiculous. We were just talking."

His expression relaxes as he rubs his arm. "I'm going to get bruises from all these times you poke at me."

"Well, don't be annoying, and I won't poke at you."

"I've told you before. It's part of my charm."

"I think you might be overestimating how charming your obnoxiousness is."

"I managed to charm you, didn't I?" Leo is leaning over toward me, his eyes almost caressing my face.

I gulp as I process the wave of deep attraction. "I could change my mind at any moment. Don't forget that."

"I won't." He presses a little kiss against my lips.

I'm expecting it this time, and it only lasts a few seconds, but it still rocks me to my foundations. I'm hot and excited and trying not to shiver as he pulls away.

Elias is watching the two of us, and I'm not sure what to make of his expression.

WHEN WE'RE BACK IN THE ROOM, getting ready for dinner, Leo asks me, "So what were you and Elias talking about earlier?"

"What?" I took a quick shower to wash off the exertion of the day and am wearing a hotel bathrobe as I do my face and hair.

"Earlier. When I went to get your drink. What were you two talking about?"

"Nothing really. I barely remember." I do remember, but I still feel weird about telling Leo. I'm not even sure why. "Why does it matter?"

"Because you wouldn't tell me and it looked…" He scowls slightly. He took a shower earlier in the afternoon, so all he had to do was change clothes. Now he's sitting in the desk chair and watching me get ready.

"It looked what?"

He shrugs and scowls again.

"Why are you being so grumpy about it? Isn't that the whole point of going on this trip? To see if he and I can…" I'm not sure why I trail off, but the rest of the words don't want to be said.

"And can you?" he asks coolly.

"I have no idea. It's only been a few days. But it's not fair of you to act like I'm betraying you by talking to your brother when this crazy scheme was your idea from the very beginning." I'm not really angry with him. I feel almost scared—like everything is about to fall apart.

Whatever Leo was feeling is pulled back inside in the space of a couple of seconds. "I know it was. I'm sorry. It just feels weird. Sometimes it feels like you're really with me, and then I see you with my brother and…"

"I know. I get it. It's kind of awkward. We're doing okay though so far. Aren't we?"

51

He meets my eyes, softening into the man I've started to know. "Yeah. We're doing just fine."

Four

THE FOLLOWING DAY, Leo announces at breakfast that he and I want to do our own thing this afternoon.

He hasn't mentioned anything to me, so I'm surprised by the declaration, especially since he's been the most easygoing of all of us so far on the trip. Since the others believe we're in the first stage of a hot romance, no one appears surprised. So we go through Mrs. Magnusson's rigorous sightseeing agenda until noon, and then we have lunch with the others, but by two in the afternoon, we're set free to do our own thing.

"What's this all about?" I ask him as we're walking away from the café where we ate lunch, the soonest I can get him alone to query him. "What did you have in mind for the afternoon?"

"Nothing really. You had to go all day yesterday, so I figured you deserved an afternoon off to do what you want."

"And the fact that your generous offer ends up getting you two afternoons off in a row is…"

"An entirely unintended outcome."

I can't help but giggle at his dry tone and twitch of a smile. Despite my teasing, I assume he really did want to get me an afternoon off and wasn't scheming for himself, so I appreciate it. "So what should we do then?"

"What do you want to do? It's your afternoon, so you get to decide."

I make a face at him. "Believe it or not, I don't care for that kind of pressure."

"What pressure? Making decisions?"

"Making decisions about what to do that affect other people. It's like when I'm expected to pick a restaurant for dinner for a whole group. I'm not a big fan of it."

He's giving me a curious look as if he's trying to figure me out. "Okay. If you were by yourself this afternoon, what would you do?"

"Honestly, probably just go back to the hotel and take a nap. I find sightseeing exhausting, and that was a big lunch. But I'm sure you'd rather do something—"

"Nap it is." He reaches over to take my hand, pulling me around the corner so we're heading in the right direction for the hotel.

"Leo!" He's walking so fast I have to jog a few steps to fall into step with him. "We don't have to nap. We can do something else relaxing like that bookstore you all did—"

"I went to the bookstore yesterday. We're napping this afternoon."

"But—"

"Lily, stop it." He gives me an impatient look. "I told you we're doing your thing this afternoon. And why the hell do you assume a nap isn't exactly what I want too?"

My scowl deepens, but it's prompted by his tone and not his words. What he's saying is actually nice.

He's still got a firm hold on my hand as we walk, and he clearly has no plans to release it anytime soon. "Well?"

"Well what?"

"I asked you a question you never answered."

I have to think back. "I assumed it was a rhetorical question."

"It wasn't. Why do you assume I don't want to take a nap too?"

"I don't really know," I admit, staying at Leo's side as he moves us out of the way of an oncoming group on the sidewalk. "It's kind of boring."

"But I'm a lazy slacker, remember? Napping is one of the things I'm good at."

I try, but I can't hold back a little laugh. His fingers tighten around mine as I do. "I don't actually think you're really lazy. You just don't like to finish things."

"Ah. Okay." He lets go of my hand and puts his palm in the middle of my back as we wait for the light to change so we can cross a street.

I like how it feels. Warm and secure. Almost protective. People looking at us casually on the street

55

almost certainly assume we're really a couple. I like that too.

When it's our time to cross, he pushes me forward gently and then takes my hand again as we cross. I'm convinced he's not conscious of what he's doing. He's not trying to make any kind of move on me. He's just navigating us through the route home in the busy city streets.

I could pull my hand out of his grip if I wanted, but I don't.

We ate lunch about a mile from the hotel, so it's not a particularly long walk back. It's not until we're making our way into the lobby that he appears to realize he's holding my hand. I see a flicker of surprise on his face before he loosens his fingers. I make sure not to be looking in his direction when he shoots me a quick glance.

He doesn't say anything about it, and neither do I.

My hand feels cold on its own. Lonely. It's ridiculous, but it's true.

When we're back up in our room, I toe off my shoes and pull off my socks, switching them out for a pair of soft, fuzzy lavender ones. After I go to the bathroom, I wash my hands and face and take off my bra. I'm wearing thick leggings and a comfortable sweater, so I don't need to change clothes to otherwise get comfortable.

On coming back into the room, I blink at the sight of a shirtless Leo, standing over his suitcase. His back is to me, but it's impossible to miss the breadth of his shoulders, the way subtle muscles ripple as he moves.

"I'm going to take a shower," he says without turning around, completely unaware of my gaping.

I manage to pull it together before he glances back at me. "Okay." I lie on top of the crisp white duvet on the bed and pull over me the small, soft throw blanket I always take on trips. "You take a lot of them."

He's on his way into the bathroom, but he pauses to look back. "What?"

"Showers. You take a lot of them. Yesterday, I think you took four. Do you always take so many?"

"No. But we're together all the time and even sleeping in the same bed. I've got to do something to relieve the tension."

I blink, momentarily clueless. My mind clearly isn't working at full capacity. I actually ask, "Because I annoy you?"

He gives a brief bark of laughter and says as he closes the bathroom door behind him, "No, you adorable little dope. Because I'm always, always turned on."

The door clicks closed before I process what he's said. Then I lie on the bed and stare at the door for a long time, my cheeks flushed and my mind buzzing.

What the hell?

He's in the shower for several minutes, and by the time I hear the water turn off, I'm not any further along with figuring things out than I was when it turned on. I have no idea what to do. What to say. What to think.

But the one thing I'm sure of is the rush of hot excitement that sparked at his words and has only gotten more intense as the minutes passed.

He comes back into the room, wearing a pair of old sweats I recognize from at least ten years ago. He's pulling on a white T-shirt as he walks.

I don't say anything, mostly because I have no idea what to say. But I can't help gazing at his body as he moves. The firm contours of his ass. The dark hair on his forearms. The way the damp hair at the nape of his neck curls just slightly.

He lies down beside me on top of the covers with a long, husky sigh. "Nap it is. An excellent idea for the afternoon."

My whole body is buzzing with interest. I can't seem to look away from him.

He turns his head in my direction. "Why are you staring at me?"

I lick my dry lips and manage to say, "When did you get so hot?" I'm not a particularly forward person, so I don't know where the question even comes from. It just comes out.

A spark ignites in his eyes. I see it happen. "Maybe I've always been this hot and you've been too clueless to see it before."

I frown slightly, taking the sardonic comment seriously. For so long, the only man I really saw was Elias. I knew Leo. Maybe better than anyone. But I'm not sure I ever really *saw* him. "Maybe so."

He clears his throat, staring up at the ceiling for a few seconds. It's like he's trying to decide what to do. Then he finally turns onto his side to face me. "I'm not going to make a move on you, Lily. When you agreed to take this trip with me, I resolved not to put any pressure on you. But just so it's clear, any hotness I possess is here for your enjoyment. Anytime you want."

My lips part slightly.

"I'm trying to be good," he adds after I don't get anything said. "But if you keep looking at me that way, I'm going to be hard-pressed not to kiss you."

"Are you being serious?" I whisper.

"What do you mean?" he asks with a frown.

"I mean are you serious? Are you being serious right now? Do you mean it?" My heart is hammering so loudly I can barely hear the sound of my own words.

He makes a choked sound. "Why would you think I'm not serious?"

"Because you have a long-standing habit of teasing me about things you don't mean. So if that's what you're doing now, then stop it. Because what would you do if I took you seriously?"

"Do you?"

"Do I...?"

"Take me seriously." His eyes are holding mine, and his expression—his whole demeanor—is captivating, intense, utterly sober.

I'm frozen for a moment with excitement and confusion both. I'm not even sure what's happening here, but something is about to. I know it for sure. "Do I take you seriously about *what* exactly?" I ask slowly, needing clarity before I give in to this.

He takes a weird little breath and doesn't answer. He also doesn't look away.

"Sex?" I prompt. "That's all you're talking about here, right?" It's very important that I get this straight. That I understand exactly what Leo is offering me right now.

Something flickers on his face. I don't understand it. But his voice is low and smooth as he murmurs, "If that's what you want from me, Lily, then that's what I'm offering."

My fast, uneven breathing is the only sound in the room. My hands are shaking beneath the blanket. "I do," I admit at last. "Want that. From you."

He rolls over on top of me before I expect it. His weight is warm and heavy and delicious. Propping himself up on his forearms, he smiles down on me. Sexy. Almost wicked. "About damn time."

"What's about damn time?" I can't help but reach up and stroke his neck and jaw. The skin is rough from his stubble, and the texture feels erotic against my palms.

"About damn time you admitted you want me."

I let out an outraged huff. "It's only been four days!"

"Four days? Lily, baby, you're hopelessly behind." He leans down to nuzzle the side of my neck. "It's been years."

I can't even begin to process what he's said because he lifts his head and kisses me. Just a featherlight brush of his lips, but it fires up all my nerve endings. It lights a fire I've never experienced before.

To say I kissed him back is an understatement. The hunger overwhelms me as I respond to the touch of his lips. I feel like I might swallow him whole.

My lips part, and I suck his tongue into my mouth. He makes a huff of sound as one of his hands slides back to hold on to my head. I'm so into the kiss that I somehow end up pushing him over onto his back and moving on top of him.

I've always enjoyed sex, and under the right circumstances I can be enthusiastic. But I've never been like this. I'm really not sure what's happening.

Leo clearly has no complaints about my eagerness. His body is tense beneath me, and I can feel his arousal hardening in his thin sweatpants. The feel of his erection against my middle drives me even wilder. I kiss him urgently and grind myself against his groin.

"Fuck," he gasps, breaking out of the kiss. His hands are moving all over me now, sliding down my back, cupping my ass over my leggings, squeezing the back of my thighs. "Fuck, Lily."

I kiss him again and try to get my hands under the waistband of his pants. I manage to get my fingers around his shaft and stroke him, making him huff and gasp again.

"Lily, I'm about to lose it here." His voice is deliciously husky. Thick. "You really want to do this? With me?"

I stare down at him, flushed and throbbing with arousal. "Yes. What the hell do you think this is about?"

"With *me*?" This time he adds emphasis, and I understand what he's really asking.

With a scowl, I pull off my sweater over my head. Since I took off my bra earlier, my breasts are completely bare beneath it.

He stares ravenously for a minute. The look really goes to my head. But then he yanks his eyes back to my face. "Thank you for that. But I still want an answer."

"Yes, Leo. With you."

With a rough burst of sound, he pulls me back down into another kiss, and this time the only thing that stops us is getting out of the rest of our clothes and pausing for him to find a condom. I'm so far gone I won't let him waste time with foreplay. It isn't long before he's rolling the condom on and I'm straddling him again, and then he's helping me position myself so I can sheathe him.

We both groan at the penetration. I flatten my hands on his chest and arch my back. Then I ride him, trying and failing to go slow. It feels too good. Soon I'm bouncing over him. A tiny part of me is watching, as if from a distance, wondering who this wild, sexy stranger is.

It's never been me before.

Leo's hands are tightly gripping my ass, holding me in position so my eager motion doesn't cause him to slip out. His eyes rake up and down from my hot face to my jiggling breasts and farther down to the place where we're joined.

I've always known him as sarcastic, laid-back, utterly unserious. I've never seen him so urgent and focused before.

It fires me up even more.

The motion itself isn't enough for me to come, so I let go with one hand so I can rub my clit.

The stimulation pushes me over the edge. I make a soft sobbing sound as an orgasm rushes through me. I shake and shudder and gasp but manage to sustain the motion. He chokes on a moan as his head tosses briefly and his features tighten.

If he's trying not to come, he doesn't succeed. His hips buck up urgently as intense pleasure washes over his face.

We slow down together until the spasms have worked their way through. Then I kind of collapse on top of him.

He strokes my long, messy hair and back. My bare butt and thighs. I gasp against his shoulder.

He's started to soften, and he slips out from the change in position so I find enough energy to move enough for him to take care of the condom.

I roll onto the bed beside him, hot and sweating and buzzing with pleasure and completely wiped out.

When he's taken care of the condom, he falls back onto the bed and pulls me over on top of him again. I have no objections. His body feels amazing right now. Warm and relaxed and softer than I've ever known him to be. I bury my face against his shoulder and breathe him in.

"Say my name," he murmurs, low and gravelly.

"Leo," I mumble without thinking, loving the sound of his name on my lips. I'm not sure why. I've just never really used his name much in the past.

Then the significance manages to pierce through the fog of satisfaction in my mind. I lift my head and frown down at him. "It was you I was fucking, Leo. You. Not your brother."

He nods with a little twitch of a smile. "Good. Just making sure."

Shaking my head, I relax again. He's got his arms around me all the way now, and it feels so good. Safe.

"We should do that again," he says after a few minutes.

"Right now?" I can't hide the surprise in my voice.

His body shakes with his soft chuckle. "Maybe not right now. But soon. We're too good together not to do this again."

"That's true."

"There's no reason we can't have a little fun on vacation," he says in his familiar light, teasing tone. "You can go back to your doomed love after that."

I shouldn't laugh at that, but I do. For some reason, my feelings for Elias don't feel as significant to me as they always did before. And it helps to hear that from Leo. Know what he's expecting from this. Sex. A good time. And nothing more. There's no pressure in that at all, which right now is a relief.

With a giggle, I reply, "It's a plan. Fun now. Doomed love later."

～

THAT EVENING, NO ONE feels very energetic, so we eat in a restaurant on the corner near the hotel. It's not late when we finish up, so while Mr. and Mrs. Magnusson head up to their room, Leo, Elias, and I hang out at a nearby bar.

It's a cool night but not cold, so we decide to sit outside. I'm perfectly comfortable in my jacket, and the fresh air feels good. Invigorating.

We're all drinking whiskey tonight. It warms me all the way down. Since this afternoon, I've been in a pleased, giggly mood—like I have a really good secret. I'm doing my best to restrain it, however. I'm not a naive teenager. I've had plenty of sex before. The fact that it was Leo I fucked shouldn't change anything.

"Next year," Elias says, taking another swallow of his drink and then leaning back in his chair. "I'm going to have to start an exercise regime a month before vacation to build up stamina for all this sightseeing."

I laugh at that, and even Leo lets out an amused huff. "I always knew I was in better shape than you."

Elias gives him the side-eye this comment deserves. "In your dreams. You had two afternoons off in a row. Tomorrow you can try to keep up with Mom while the rest of us take it easy."

Leo slides his arm across the back of my chair. It's a casual, possessive gesture I can't help but like even though he's probably not even aware he's doing it. "I'm sure we can schedule in a nap for you if you need it."

Elias doesn't reply to this. Just shoots his brother another mild glare.

"I'm looking forward to the beach next week," I say. "Mostly to get some rest. Where do you think she's taking us?"

Leo shrugs, and Elias says, "There's no telling. I've never been disappointed in her choice for the beach week though."

I glance up at Leo to see what he's thinking.

"Me either," he murmurs, giving my long braid a tug. "Whatever it is, it will be good."

"We never did much in the way of family vacations," I say, leaning back against his arm, liking how it feels.

"None at all?" Elias asks.

"You went on trips," Leo adds with a frown. "I'm sure I remember you going out of town."

"We did some. I mean, when I was a kid, they took me to the beach once, but otherwise all our trips were culturally improving and not about having fun. They really felt more like a job than a vacation." I snort as I think back. "One year, they took me on a musical tour of Germany. Three cities in one week. Six concerts. And a lot of pressure on me to be equally brilliant."

"That sounds hard," Elias murmurs. His eyes are on me. He's seeing me. Hearing me. Feeling for me. I know it for sure.

I give my head a little shake as I smile dryly. "I definitely didn't enjoy most of our trips. They meant well. They love me… as well as they know how." I add the last words to be truthful, not to earn any sympathy. "I've had it way better than a lot of people, so I don't mean to sound like I'm whining. It's just new to me. To be on a family vacation like this."

"Where would you go if you had the choice?" Elias asks. "Out of anywhere in the world."

"I… don't really know." I shift in my chair. Leo's arm is across my shoulder now.

"Yes, you do," he says. "You thought of something just now. What is it?"

I make a face at him.

"Tell me."

"Don't be pushy," Elias says. "If she doesn't want to share, she doesn't have to."

Leo starts to respond, but I talk over him, not wanting it to turn into even a mild argument. "It's not a secret or anything," I say. "It's just not that exciting. I've always loved the Anne of Green Gables books, and I used to dream of visiting Prince Edward Island. I would always ask my parents if we could go, and they'd say maybe someday. But we never went."

"So why don't you go now?" Elias asks.

"I will. One day. I just haven't gotten there yet." For some reason, I feel kind of embarrassed. Like I shared too much of my soul.

It's silly. I didn't share anything intimate. Just a little dream I've had all my life. Like receiving the single lily as the perfect romantic gesture. A small personal thing. Not a big deal.

Leo moves his hand under my hair so he's gently rubbing my neck. It feels so good I want to moan.

I don't, of course.

When I look across the table, I catch Elias watching Leo with a strangely intense scrutiny. Curious, I glance up at Leo. His eyes were on me, but they move away as soon as I meet them.

My stomach twists with a discomfort I don't understand. I'm not sure what all these looks are about, but they make me feel weird. Like there are silent conversations going on over my head that I'm being left out of.

I take another sip of my whiskey and close my eyes as it hits my mouth, my throat, all the way down.

"Did you want to be a professional musician?" Elias asks out of the blue.

It's such an unexpected question that I'm not even sure he's speaking to me until I see his eyes on my face. "I don't know. I mean, I guess? I've always loved music, and I always wanted to spend my life doing it. My parents had in mind for me to be a concert pianist. Or a composer. Someone really great. But I was never that good."

"You always seemed pretty good to me."

"Thanks for that," I say, smiling at Elias. "Seriously. I'm good, but not great. My parents wanted a genius."

"And you're not one?" Elias's question appears to be a genuine one.

I can't help but laugh. "No. Sadly, no genius here. Just some basic talent and a love for music. I love teaching. I'm good at it. I'd rather not have the pressure of being a genius, if you want to know the truth."

"That makes sense. Were your parents disappointed?"

I'm not sure how to answer that. The truth, as I've told Leo more than once before, is that they're definitely disappointed in me. But it doesn't feel like something I should admit to Elias. It might come across like I'm looking for sympathy when I'm not.

"Maybe a little, but they're fine with it now. They do their thing, and I do mine. We've never been close like you all are. No family vacations for us."

Leo is still gently massaging my neck. "You can join our vacations anytime you want."

I'm not sure if he's teasing or not, so I have to check his face. Even after checking, I'm not sure.

"I agree," Elias adds. "Since otherwise I'll have no one but Leo to hang out with."

I laugh at that, and the mood breaks. Talk is friendly and casual after that.

I'M NOT A SERIOUS BATH PERSON as a rule, but the tub in our hotel room is really nice, and they've provided some lovely lavender-honey bath oil that's very tempting. Leo had to stop by his parents' room on our way up for some reason, so I get back to the room on my own and decide to take a bath.

Often baths for me don't live up to their hype, but this one is just as nice as I was hoping. Warm and relaxing and fragrant.

I've been soaking for about ten minutes when I hear Leo come into the room. "Lily?" he calls through the closed bathroom door.

"Yeah. I'm in here. I'm taking a bath."

"Okay." He opens the bathroom door and comes in.

"Hey! I didn't say you could come in." Foolishly, I try to hide my breasts with my arms. I'm fully submerged in the water and there are some light bubbles from the oil, but I'm still very conscious of my nakedness.

"I need to brush my teeth," he explains with an amused expression that proves he knows exactly what he's doing.

"And you couldn't wait a few more minutes."

"Nope. Bad breath. Can't be tolerated." He flashes me a little smile.

"Asshole. Go ahead and brush your teeth. But keep your eyes to yourself."

"You let me see you naked this afternoon."

"That was different."

"How was it different?"

"That was sex. This is a bath. Nakedness is different in different contexts."

"Ah. Got it." He puts toothpaste on his brush and sticks it in his mouth. I watch him brush, and it feels strange. Domestic. Intimate.

I swish the water around and feel a tightness in my gut clench harder.

To his credit, Leo doesn't stare at me. He brushes his teeth and splashes water on his face. Then he pulls off his shirt.

I watch him as he changes into his pajamas. He's obviously doing it in the bathroom so I'll watch. I can't help but enjoy it although he's not making a show of it.

"What were you talking to your parents about?" I ask after he's done.

He blinks, looking blank for just a moment. "What? Oh, just now? Nothing important. Just logistical stuff."

Logistics aren't particularly interesting to me, so I don't pursue it.

He comes over and kneels down beside the tub.

"What are you doing?" I ask, staring up at him, my heart starting to speed up.

He leans over to kiss me—light, teasing.

That same blaze of passion overtakes me. Fires up immediately at the touch of his lips. I grab for his head and kiss him harder. He smiles against my mouth.

"What are you smirking at?" I demand.

"I'm not smirking. I'm smiling."

"It felt like a smirk to me."

"Well, it wasn't. I just like the way you respond when I kiss you."

All my female parts clench hard. "How do I respond?"

"Like you're dying of thirst, and I'm a drink of water." There's a thick, teasing note in his tone that's utterly irresistible.

I splash water at him with a huff. "I'm not that bad!"

"You're not bad at all. You're very, very good." His hand trails into the water, teasing my taut nipples.

I have to bite my bottom lip so I don't groan out loud from the sparks of pleasure from his touch.

"Look at you," he murmurs, caressing from my breasts down toward my groin. "You want me to touch you so badly."

It's true, but a stubborn streak inside me doesn't want to admit it. I rock my hips up and grip the edge of the tub to keep from grabbing his hand and moving it where I need to feel it.

"You're already turned on."

"Not that turned on," I manage to say, although my blazing cheeks and panting breath and clenched fingers all belie the words.

"You're so turned on you can hardly hold yourself back." There's a smile in his voice but not an obnoxious one. "What's it going to take to push you over the edge?"

It's a challenge. I know one when I hear one. So I do my best to control the throbbing need he's awakened in my body. He takes his time, teasing my body in the water. Tweaking my nipples. Rubbing my inner thighs. Skating his fingertips across the sensitive spots at the crook in my neck.

My grip on the edges of the tub gets tighter and tighter. My chest is heaving from my ragged breathing. My eyes are clenched shut, but that means every place he touches me is a surprise.

"Let me see it, Lily."

"See what?"

"The real you break out of the controlled person you try to be."

"I don't—" I cut off the argument with a choked cry as he tweaks my nipples again.

"Let me see her, Lily." He walks his fingers down my belly, and I squeak when he reaches my groin. He opens me with his hand and gives my clit a quick flick.

I make a helpless sound and arch up.

He flicks it again, and I actually come.

From nothing more than that.

"There she is," he rasps as my body shakes through the unexpected spasms. "The real Lily. You're the hottest little thing I've ever known."

I give up after that. I grab for him, practically climbing up his body as he pulls me out of the tub.

He carries me to the bed, and he's all over me. He uses his hands and mouth until I come hard and then come again. Then he turns me over and takes me from behind until I'm stifling sobs of pleasure into the covers. He loses control then and comes himself, but a couple of hours later he's up for more.

We go at it on and off all night until we're limp and exhausted. Even near the end, every time he kisses me, that same fire ignites inside me.

The one that burns and burns and always wants more.

Five

THE REST OF THE WEEK goes quickly—filled with sightseeing and good food and lots and lots of sex.

On Saturday morning, I'm packing up for the trip to the next stage of our vacation. I still have no idea where we're going, and I don't even care. It's a beach destination, so it will be warm and sunny and relaxing. There's no way it's not going to be good.

Leo got mostly packed last night, and this morning he got up early enough to take a run. He's still not back, but I'm not particularly worried. For someone as unhurried as he is by nature, he can shower and get dressed remarkably quickly.

I'm trying to organize my suitcase into some semblance of neatness when I hear the hotel room door open and then close.

"We're supposed to leave for the airport in less than thirty minutes," I call out without even turning around. "So you better get your ass moving."

"My ass is moving just fine." The low voice comes from right behind me, so close I actually jump. "You certainly had no complaints about the way it moved last night."

My body clenches with excitement, but I've always believed it was a bad idea to indulge the male ego. So I roll my eyes and keep my gaze on my folded leggings. "Your ass does an adequate job most of the time, as does the rest of your body. But at the moment, it needs to get a move on since I don't want us to be responsible for the entire family being late for the flight."

"It's a private jet. They're not going to leave without us."

"It's the principle of the thing." I turn around because I simply can't resist the husky note in his voice. Then I blink when I see the perspiration dripping down his face. "How do you get so sweaty when it's this cold outside?"

"I'm uniquely talented." His mouth quirks up in the most adorable half smile.

I try (and fail) not to return the smile. "Well, you're a mess. Go take a shower."

He reaches out to take my face in both hands, but before he can lean into a kiss, I pull back. "Don't you dare get me all sweaty!" His shirt is soaked through, and his hair is sticking to his face and neck.

"What's wrong with getting a little sweaty. You didn't complain—"

"I know, I know. I didn't complain when we got sweaty before. But I'm all dressed and ready to go this morning, and I'm not going to redo it all for a quickie."

He leans over again within an inch of my mouth, but he doesn't actually kiss me. "It doesn't have to be a quickie."

"Yes, it does. I don't like to be late when it means other people have to wait for us. Go get in the shower." I turn him around and give him a little shove toward the bathroom.

He goes without resistance, although I can hear him grumbling about my bossiness as he goes.

I can't help but giggle, although I manage to wait until he closes the door so he can't hear me since he likes it when he can make me laugh.

I never spent much time imagining what Leo would be like in a sexual relationship, but he's definitely surprised me this week. Not that he's good in bed but that it's softened him so much. He's still himself. Smart and sarcastic and quick to argue and bone dry in his humor. He still has a particular talent for getting on my nerves, and he doesn't take much of anything serious. But he's also surprisingly thoughtful. Observant. Considerate. I've never had better sex in my life, and I've been enjoying him as much out of bed as in.

If we hadn't made it clear that this is sex with no strings, my emotions might have been getting a bit confused. But so far I'm doing well in keeping things in perspective. I've never had a relationship like this before, but it's strangely freeing. To indulge myself without worrying about consequences. Without getting hung up on what it all means or what's going to happen a month from now or a year from now.

I've got two more weeks left of this vacation, and I'm determined to enjoy every day. I want it to be good, whether Elias ends up noticing me at all.

~

WE FLY TO SAINT LUCIA in the Caribbean, and I'm thrilled with the luxury resort and the gorgeous suites with private infinity pools overlooking panoramic views of the mountains and sea. I've never stayed anywhere like this before, and the fact that I have a week of it is enough to make me hug myself.

I catch Leo giving me a side-eye as the bellman shows us around our suite, and I assume he's laughing at my visible excitement. But I'm not a sophisticated person, and how the hell does someone keep from conveying how happy this kind of rare indulgence makes them?

As soon as we're alone, I announce I'm going to jump in our own private pool. I've got my clothes off and am starting to pull on my bathing suit when he grabs me and throws me onto the bed.

Squealing with surprise and laughter, I try to get away, claiming I want the pool more than sex (which is not remotely true). He retaliates by tickling me. I've always prided myself on having a strong tolerance for tickling, but Leo manages to overcome that knack without even trying. I laugh until I cry as we roll around on the bed, but as soon as I say, "Enough," he stops.

He's grinning full out as he props himself up above me. His eyes are deeply warm—not just hot. "Now then. What do you have to say for yourself?"

"Asshole," I rasp, still giggling a little.

He nuzzles my neck. "You're really pushing your luck here, baby."

"What am I supposed to say?"

"You're supposed to admit that sex with me is better than a dip in the pool."

"Well, sex with you is pretty damn good. But that pool looks exceptional."

He narrows his eyes.

I can't resist. I wrap my arms around his neck and pull him down into a brief hug. "I'd insist on the pool first, just to have my way. But pools are a little bit drying, so sex afterward might not be entirely comfortable. So what do you say to sex first and then the pool?"

He murmurs right against my lips, "I say that's sounds exactly right."

THE FOLLOWING MORNING, I'm finishing a mimosa on the terrace of Mr. and Mrs. Magnusson's suite. It overlooks the water, just like mine and Leo's, but it has a larger table that fits all of us. We had a delicious breakfast of eggs, fruit, and crepes, and we've been lingering at the table for more than an hour—enjoying the sun, the salty breeze, and the beautiful ocean view.

I'm not sure why, but I'm so happy this morning it feels like I could melt into the bench I'm sharing with Leo. It's not just the luxury accommodations or the setting. It's feeling like part of this family as they laugh and bicker and make plans.

I never felt like this with my own family. Not even once.

Leo and Elias are arguing about whether to take a jungle hike tomorrow or take a boat out for the day. Both options sound great to me, so I haven't bothered weighing in.

"Let's let Lily decide," Elias says at last. "Since we're evenly split."

"She doesn't like making those kinds of decisions," Leo says with a quick glance toward me.

He says it before I can say it myself. I blink at him in surprise.

"You just say that because you know she'll take my side." Elias flashes me a devastating smile. "Right, Lily?"

"Not right. But I don't take anyone's side. I'm happy either way, and if we really want to avoid the conflict, we can do one tomorrow and the other on Tuesday or Wednesday. We've got all week, right?"

Both guys look rather stumped at that piece of logic, and Mr. Magnusson chuckles before returning to whatever he's reading on his phone.

"Let's go talk to Victor," Elias says, referring to the resort's concierge and giving his brother a soft punch on the shoulder. "We can see what he thinks about the best day to do what and make all the reservations we need."

So Leo and Elias get up, Elias ready for a mission and Leo clearly more reluctant to get moving. Then Mr. Magnusson heads back inside to use the bathroom, and Mrs. Magnusson and I are left alone.

I don't mind. I'm comfortable with her now. I really like her.

"This place is beautiful," I tell her. "Thank you so much for choosing it."

"It is rather nice, isn't it? And there's no need to thank me for anything. I should be thanking you."

My mouth turns into a slight frown. "Thank me? For what?"

"For Leo." Her eyes move to the door inside where Leo and Elias disappeared a few minutes ago. "I haven't seen him so happy in…" She shakes her head and spreads her hands. "Honestly, I don't remember ever seeing him so happy."

I gulp, taken aback and not knowing what to say. "Oh. I mean… Oh. I guess he's having a pretty good time."

She laughs uninhibitedly. "A pretty good time? Surely you're not so blind. He's happier than I've ever seen him, and I know perfectly well it's because of you."

I shift in my seat. Bite my lip. Try not to squirm. "Oh."

She reaches over to pat my hand on the table. "I didn't mean to embarrass you. I know you two are just starting out. But I've always worried about that boy. He's always had such a good heart, but he never felt comfortable showing it to anyone. It's like he believed he had to hide it in order to protect it. I often wondered if he ever would let go of it. I'm so glad it's you who has finally brought it out."

My cheeks are blazing. I'm not capable of saying a single word, but fortunately Mrs. Magnusson doesn't expect me to respond.

She pats my hand again with another soft laugh. "I'm sorry, dear. I'm sure this is completely inappropriate, and Leo would give me a firm lecture if he knew I was saying this. But I'm so happy to see him happy. I'm sure you understand."

"Yes. I understand."

I do. I understand exactly where she's coming from, but it's not just embarrassment that I'm feeling.

It's guilt.

Guilt.

Because she thinks Leo has found a woman to love, but he hasn't.

He's only found me.

MRS. MAGNUSSON PLANNED Sunday as a lazy day, so we're able to hang out on the beach or at the pool all day, breaking only to take naps or eat meals.

After a late lunch, Leo and I are getting settled into a private cabana at the beach. It's equipped with a comfortable double lounge with cushions and a drink cooler and curtains that can be pulled all the way.

I've never been to the beach like this before. It's a surreal experience. I'm wearing a cute red two-piece. Only moderately revealing, but I still feel ridiculously sexy as I stretch out on the lounge. The breeze is perfect and so is the shade from the cabana since my fair skin doesn't do well with too much direct sun.

I smile up at Leo, who's pulling his T-shirt off over his head, mussing his hair in the process.

"I'm going to take a swim," he says, leaning over to see me better. "You want to come?"

"Not right now. I'm full from lunch and too comfortable to get wet. You shouldn't do any heavy swimming right now after that meal."

"I'm not going to do a lot of swimming. Just get wet. I won't be long."

"Take your time. I'm going to take a nap."

I've never once fallen asleep on the beach, but I've also never been so comfortable. I smooth my hair and settle my sunglasses and then close my eyes and relax.

So far, I haven't had a single complaint about the day, except it's passing too fast.

Leo is only in the water for about ten minutes. When he returns, he flings some water on me—enough to be his normal obnoxious self but not enough for me to get upset about. Then he dries off and stretches out on the lounge beside me.

"How's the nap going?" he asks, turning his head toward me. His face is about three inches away from mine.

"It had barely gotten started before you flung water all over me." I wipe a stray drop from my belly with a disapproving frown. "What if I was asleep?"

"I knew you weren't asleep."

"How did you know that? You can't see my eyes behind the sunglasses."

"I've seen you when you sleep every night for more than a week now. I know when you're asleep."

"How do you know?"

He just gives me a smug smile as he puts on his own sunglasses.

With a faint snarl, I prompt, "How?"

"Maybe you snore."

"I do not snore." I'm pretty sure this is true, but I still add after a moment, "Do I?"

"No," he admits with a chuckle. "You don't snore. But you do clutch the blankets when you sleep."

"What?"

"You clutch the blankets." He takes the end of his towel and lays it over my stomach and then positions my hand on top of it. Then he curls my fingers into the fabric in a tight clench. "Like that. Always with your right hand and not your left. Like you're hanging on in your sleep."

My mouth falls open slightly. "I don't do that."

"Yes, you do." His voice is warm and affectionate, but I can't see his eyes behind the dark lenses. "Every night. You put your one hand on top of the covers and you hang on to it."

I always knew I preferred to keep one hand out of the covers, but I had no idea I did this. "Maybe that's why my hand sometimes cramps up."

"That would be a good bet. You need to learn to let go a little."

"I can let go."

"Can you? It seems to me that you always want to keep control of things. Even in your sleep you're trying to hang on."

"I can't help what I do in my sleep. And I'm not that controlling. I don't try to boss people around or always be in charge. I really don't."

"You certainly try to boss me around."

"That's different. That's because you need some herding. But with most people, I don't."

"You know what I think?" He's moved even closer, and one of his hands is now covering mine over the piece of his towel that's still draped over me.

My cheeks are flushing, and I really don't know why. "Do you think I want to know what you think?"

"Probably not. But I'm going to tell you anyway. The way you are with other people is learned behavior. You've trained yourself to step back into the shadows. But the person you are with me is who you really are."

I gulp. Can't even breathe for a moment.

"Aren't you?" he asks, his voice a sensual caress.

"I... don't know."

"Don't you?"

"No. I've never thought about it before, and I don't know if that's true or not. I have other friends besides you, you know. I act like myself with them too."

"Sure. But only parts of yourself. The parts that you think are most acceptable. Not the bossy, controlling neurotic who desperately tries to keep a grip on the world even in her sleep."

I jerk away, all my soft yearning shifting into hurt.

"Oh my God, baby, that's not an insult." He moves until he's propped up over me. He cups my face.

"You just called me bossy and controlling and a neurotic. How is that not an insult?"

"Because I like bossy, controlling neurotics." He's smiling with that soft expression again. The one I didn't even know he was capable of two weeks ago. "Why else would I have chosen you for my fake girlfriend?"

I make a face at him, but I'm not offended anymore. It's impossible not to believe him when he's looking at me that way. "You chose me because I was convenient."

He shakes his head, his expression shifting. "Believe me, that's not it. Nothing could be less convenient than taking a vacation with a woman who's in love with my brother."

The reference to Elias is like a kick in the gut. And it's followed by a wave of intense confusion. Because the truth is I haven't been thinking about Elias for the past week. Almost at all. I've talked to him more than I ever have before, and I feel like he knows me a lot better than he did. But I'm not daydreaming about him. Or visualizing his face when I close my eyes. A lot of the time, I completely forget what the point of this ludicrous scheme really is.

It's strange. Unnerving. And terrifying in a way I can't fully process.

Leo has filled the hollow places in my heart so completely that there's barely room for Elias there at all.

If he were a different person, I wouldn't mind. I'd be happy about the change. But Leo hasn't really changed even though we know each other intimately now. And the one thing that's always been true about him is that he doesn't take anything seriously. He's not a closer.

He just can't stick the landing.

So while he obviously likes me and is having a good time with me, he hasn't forgotten about the purpose of our plan the way I have. He assumes I still love Elias and that the sex we're having is casual.

No strings.

He's right about me. I'm always holding on. And evidently the string I've started to hold on to now is Leo's.

I've hurt myself enough by indulging a doomed love for half my life. I don't want to hurt myself again— even more—by hoping for something to happen with Leo.

So I do some quick mental gymnastics until I feel like I have appropriate perspective again. "I guess that's probably true," I tell him with a little smile. "But to go back to our previous topic, I'm not the only one with strange sleeping habits. For instance, you always stick one foot out of the covers."

He chuckles and rolls back to settle beside me. "I know that. But there's a good reason for that. I get hot, and it's temperature control."

"Uh-huh."

"If you think about it, both of us are who we really are when we sleep."

His voice has that teasing note I recognize, but I can't follow the logic. "What do you mean?"

"I mean, when you're asleep, you have to hang on, and that's who you really are. And when I'm asleep…"

"Oh my God, don't even say it."

He leans up to give me a quick kiss. "When I'm asleep, I'm smoking hot."

After dinner, I take a bath in the huge soaking tub and then change into a pretty blue gown. It's in a soft, comfortable knit material that skims over my body in a way I like, and it's the nicest piece of nightwear I brought with me.

The moon and stars are bright outside, and the air is still pleasantly warm, so I pour myself a glass of wine from the bottle Leo brought up from dinner and take it out to the terrace to drink it.

I stretch out in a lounge chair and sip the wine, feeling relaxed and self-indulgent in a way I usually don't feel. Leo was in the shower when I came outside, but I assume he'll probably come and join me eventually.

That will be nice.

I'm smiling to myself over the rim of my wineglass as I stare out at the ocean at night, the starlight glinting off the gentle waves.

"Have you had a good day?" His voice surprises me even though I've been expecting him.

"Yeah. I really have. This is an amazing place."

"It is nice. My mom did great in picking this year."

"I don't know how I can ever thank you all for bringing me along. I know it wasn't the point, but you've pretty much given me the vacation of a lifetime."

Leo gives a half shrug. He's wearing nothing but a pair of thin cotton pajama pants in a light gray color. He's got a glass of wine too, and he settles into the lounge beside mine. "We'd already arranged for Penny to come, so we would have lost money if no one took her place."

"I guess so. But I still really appreciate it. I've been having a good time despite the weirdness."

"I'm glad." He's smiling as he sips his merlot. It's not his normal ironic smile, and it's not directed at me. It's private, like he's smiling only to himself. "I have no complaints about the trip so far either."

I experience a soft, unsettled clench in my chest and belly, and it makes me decidedly nervous. So I cover the confusion the way I usually do. "That's because you're getting a lot of sex."

Leo lets out a soft, amused breath. "That's definitely a bonus." He gives me a quick, sidelong glance. "But I'd be having a good time without it."

"Me too."

We sit in silence for several minutes until we've finished our wine. It's not awkward or uncomfortable. The silence feels companionable. Like we're both on the same page.

Eventually I feel so good that I stretch my arms and back, closing my eyes as the warm breeze wafts over my bare skin. When I glance over again, I see Leo's eyes are on me. His expression has changed.

Even in the faint light, I know what the look in his eyes means. "We had sex after lunch," I say.

"Yes. And your point is?"

"We don't really need to have sex again now."

"Did I say anything?"

"You had your sex look going."

"My sex look?"

"Yes. It's a horny kind of look. I know it well." I'm trying to keep my tone dry, but I really feel like giggling, and my body is already reacting in anticipation.

"Since when do we have sex only once a day?"

"Never," I admit. "But technically we've already had sex twice today since you got going again after midnight last night. Surely twice is enough to satisfy you."

"It's not." He starts to reach out toward me but pauses midgesture. "Unless you really don't feel like it?"

I laugh. "I guess maybe I could summon up the energy." I start to get up off my lounge.

"Where are you going?"

"I was going inside. Weren't we just talking about having sex?"

"Why can't we stay right here?"

I blink and glance around. The terrace is private, lush, gilded with the white moonlight. "We're outside."

"No one can see us."

"But they might be able to hear us. Plus you're kind of energetic in bed. You think that lounge is going to hold up?"

"I think it can handle it." He pulls me down on top of him so I'm straddling his lap. "And you're always pretty quiet."

I frown as I stroke his chest with the palms of both hands. "I'm not that quiet."

He's smiling as he pulls my gown off over my head, leaving me naked to the open air. "You don't want to be quiet, but you're always stifling your sounds."

"No, I don't." I'm briefly distracted by the question. "Do I?"

His body shakes with soft, fond laughter. He cups my breasts with his hands. "Yes, you do. I told you you're always trying to stay in control."

"I don't mean to. I don't know why I would do that." I arch my back when he teases my nipples with his thumbs. "I guess it's not very sexy."

"Lily, don't be ridiculous. You can be as quiet as you want. You can bite your lip as much as you need. You're still going to be the sexiest thing I've ever known."

I open my eyes to check his face. I see that same warm amusement there but also sincerity. Like he means it.

"Besides," he adds, "I take it as a challenge." He lifts my body until he can take one breast in his mouth. "One day I'm going to make you scream."

"Don't..." I gasp at the surge of pleasure that slices through me as he teases my nipple with his tongue. "...count on it."

He kisses and caresses me until I'm whimpering and can't stay still. I try to do the same for him, but he keeps distracting me. Eventually I give up and let him work me up to a state of intense arousal. Then he penetrates me with two fingers, and I'm so far gone I eagerly ride his hand.

My whole body jiggles with my urgency. I'm panting and huffing and starting to sweat. I'd be embarrassed by my uninhibited performance if I weren't aware of Leo gazing at me hotly the whole time with a possessiveness that's impossible to miss. When I realize I'm biting my lip to smother the sounds I'm making, I consciously try to unclench.

I make the strangest sound as I bounce on top of him. It's raw and primal and louder than I usually am.

"There you go," he murmurs thickly, adjusting his hand to give me better access. "That's right, baby. Let go. I've got you. You can let it go."

I come then—before I know to expect it—and make another loud, helpless sound as the spasms of pleasure crash through me. I keep moving over him until the orgasm has worked through me and I'm limp and panting.

He's smiling up at me as he finally retrieves his hand from between my legs. "Hottest thing I've ever known," he murmurs.

The words fill me with almost as much satisfaction as the physical sensations. I reach for the condom he brought with him—I hadn't noticed it when he first got here—and tear it open. After pushing down his pants, I roll the condom on over his full erection. Then he helps me position myself over him, sheathing him with my body.

He groans at the penetration, his hands tight on the bare skin of my ass. Then I start to ride him again, and it's even better this time because he's bucking up into my motion with thrusts of his own.

It doesn't take long before both of us are coming hard and crying out at the moment of completion. He's louder than I am—he obviously doesn't care about who might hear—but I do try not to smother the sound the way I normally do.

He seems quite pleased with the whole situation, and I'm almost proud of myself as I collapse on top of him afterward.

He strokes my long, loose hair and my bare back and bottom. "That was amazing, baby."

"Yeah. Yeah." That's all I can articulate at the moment.

"You don't have to prove anything to me, Lily. I meant what I said. Scream or don't scream—whatever you want. I'm always going to think you're the best thing that's ever happened to me."

That's not exactly what he said earlier, and I lift my head so I can scan his face. He's got his eyes closed. He looks like he's almost asleep. I don't think he has any idea what he just said to me.

He just had very good sex. Men often say things they don't mean in bed. He was talking about hot sex. Nothing more.

I'm not going to read into it.

One doomed love in a lifetime is more than enough.

Six

THE REST OF THE WEEK passes in much the same manner. Plenty of sun, relaxation, tropical drinks, good food, and sex. We do both the jungle hike and go out on a boat one day, but that is the extent of the planned activities.

It's one of the best weeks I've ever had.

Waking up on Friday morning, I'm aware of an ache of regret in my stomach—the one I always feel when something really good is coming to an end. Naturally, we have next week, and hopefully that will be good too. But after that the vacation is over. Then I'll have to go back to the real world.

Right now the real world doesn't seem all that appealing. Leo and I might return to what we were before. It was good. I can see now that he always brought a certain kind of light to my life with his sharp, glinting self. But I like him a lot better now, and I don't want to lose him.

My yearning for Elias is a fuzzy memory at the moment. It makes me feel weird and kind of embarrassed. Sometimes I wonder if the feelings will all come back to me after we get home, after I'm no longer in Leo's bed.

Right now it seems impossible, but I'm having trouble seeing past the present.

I've been sleeping on my back. Gripping the covers with my right hand as usual. I tuck that arm back under the sheet and turn over onto my side to face Leo's side of the bed.

He's still there. It's early. The sun hasn't even started to rise yet.

Maybe it's my motion, or maybe it's just that time of the morning, but Leo begins to wake up too. He sniffs and jerks and opens his eyes, blinking a few times before he focuses on me. "Hey."

"Hi."

"Why are you awake?"

"I don't know. I just woke up. It's too early to get up though."

"Yeah." He lets out a breath and rubs his hair with one hand, making it even messier than it was.

"Isn't it time for your run?" He's still been getting up early to run most mornings.

"I might skip it today. Take a day off." He reaches out and pulls me against him, wrapping both arms around me. "Staying in bed sounds a lot better."

"That's for sure, but if you've got sex in mind, you can forget it. I need to recover from last night." He smells warm and natural—like Leo—and I breathe him in.

"So do I," he admits with a soft chuckle. He slides one hand up my back until it's cradling my head. "We can take it easy this morning."

"Excellent plan." I've wrapped my arms around his middle, mostly because there's nothing else to do with my hands. But it feels comfortable and secure, lying in bed with him like this.

I wonder if he likes it as much as I do.

He's the one who initiated it, so I have to assume he wants to hold me like this. I'm pressed up against his front, both of us on our sides, and I slide one of my legs against his. I can feel his leg hair. It's rougher than my skin. He really is in very good shape, but he's got a little softness on his sides that's fun to squeeze.

We lie together like that until I doze off again. He must have fallen asleep too because when I wake up again, he's on his back and I'm sprawled half on top of him. His body is hot and relaxed, and his breathing is slow and even. I lift my head to orient myself and discover that his eyes are open. "Oh."

"Oh what?" he asks.

"You're awake."

"I was asleep. I woke up a few minutes ago."

"Oh." I put my head back down, resting my cheek against his chest since it's as comfortable as anywhere else. "What time is it?"

"After eight now."

Something in the air feels different now. It makes my chest feel heavy. I glance back up at his face but can't read anything there. "What are you thinking about?" I ask, since asking is the only way I'll ever know.

"I was thinking about whether you think you've gotten Elias to notice you yet."

97

It's not at all what I might have expected to hear from him. And definitely not what I was wanting to hear—although I'm not sure I could articulate what I do want. I put my head back down and shift positions, giving myself a few seconds before I answer. "Oh. Why were you thinking about that?"

"We're two weeks in now. After today, there's only one week left of the trip. Are you disappointed by how things have gone?"

"You know I'm not disappointed. I've been having a great time."

"Sure, but you went on the trip because you wanted Elias to fall in love with you." He pauses, idly wrapping his finger around a thick bunch of my hair. "Do you not want that anymore?"

When faced with the direct question, I feel trapped. Frozen. He's put into words the source of my confusion, and I don't have a definite answer for him. "I... don't really know," I say at last.

"Why don't you know?"

"Well, it's kind of hard to think about it when I'm having all this sex with you." That's true enough, and it seems safer than admitting anything else.

"Yeah. I guess that's probably true. Should we take a break from sex today so you can think about it?" He sounds light. Casual. Almost amused. Not angsty or upset or anything that would prove he was feeling something deeply. "Wouldn't want you to miss your chance with Elias."

It's what I've always known to expect from it, but it still makes my heart drop painfully. "Sure. If that's what you want."

"I'm always going to want to have sex with you, Lily. You know that. But I want you to get what you want. And I don't want you to blame me if you don't."

"I wouldn't blame you." I still feel weird. Like something is not quite right. But Leo is making things very clear right now, and he wants me to have a chance with Elias.

It's actually a kind gesture. He doesn't want me to miss out on what I really want even if that means less sex for him.

So I shouldn't feel crushed about it—like he's passing me off to his brother now that he's had his fill of me.

He's never taken things seriously in life, so it's not like he's going to take *me* seriously.

He's still holding my hair in his hand. He hasn't let it go.

EVERYONE SEEMS RATHER tired today. We have a late breakfast together and sit around for a long time, sometimes talking and sometimes not.

I've been finishing my second cup of coffee and staring out at the view. Leo is sitting beside me reading a newspaper while Elias and his father are across the table, scrolling through their phones. Mrs. Magnusson has gone inside to shower and dress.

No one appears to want to do much of anything, and that's just fine with me.

Elias finally puts down his phone with a sigh. He hasn't shaved yet today. He rubs his jaw with one hand. "I guess I should probably do something."

"Why?" Leo asks from behind the newspaper. "Take it easy like the rest of us."

"I feel like moving a little. I'm going to take a walk on the beach." He stands up, pulling down his T-shirt since it's gotten hiked up. "Anyone want to come?"

"Not me," Mr. Magnusson says. "I ate too much breakfast."

"Me too," Leo says.

I'm about to agree since I usually do what Leo does, but then I remember our conversation this morning.

I'm supposed to be figuring out my feelings for Elias, and that's not going to happen unless I spend a little time with him. A walk seems easy and natural enough. No one will think it's weird or inappropriate.

So I say, "I'll go if you don't mind. I could stretch my legs."

"Sure." Elias smiles, making it clear I'm welcome, and then glances over at Leo.

Leo lowers the paper and scans my face quickly. For a moment I think he's going to decide to join us, but he must realize what's on my mind. He lifts the newspaper again and says casually, "You've got more energy than I do. Have fun."

With this decided, I stop to use the bathroom quickly and pull my hair into a braid since it's windy on the beach. Then I meet Elias outside and we walk together toward the water.

We talk occasionally about casual things and sometimes don't talk at all, but it feels friendly enough. Not like we're really close but like we're used to each other. We go far enough that we decide to take a rest. Elias buys us both a lemonade, and we sit on a bench to drink it.

It's another beautiful day. We haven't had anything else here. I'm going to miss this place when we leave tomorrow.

I wonder what Leo is doing right now.

As if he read my mind, Elias says, "Is Leo okay today?"

"What do you mean?"

"I don't know. He just seemed a little... off. Or something. Things are still fine between you two?" He's taken off his sunglasses, and Elias's eyes look very blue in the bright sunlight as he focuses them on me.

"Yes. Things are fine." I don't know what else to say. I certainly can't tell him the whole truth. "He's fine."

"Good." He glances away, out toward where the sea and sky meet in a bright haze. "I never would have pictured you two together before, but you've really been good for him."

I feel my cheeks warming. His mother said something similar. Maybe, maybe it's really true. Maybe in some unexpected way, I'm good for Leo.

And he's good for me too.

Elias catches my eyes again. "I hope it works out."

And that's the moment. When it all becomes perfectly clear.

The man beside me is every bit as handsome and smart and cool as he ever was—with fascinating layers hiding beneath his composure and a kindness at the core of him. But I don't love him.

I was holding on to the dream of him—refusing to let it go—because it represented something in my mind that I've always yearned for. Love. Connection. Fellowship.

Home.

But it wasn't really Elias I wanted, and I've found what I need in someone else.

The realization rocks me. I clench my trembling hands together.

"You okay?" Elias asks in a softer voice.

I nod and give him a shaky smile. "Yeah. Things are just starting out with Leo. I don't really… I don't really know what will happen."

"I know. And I'm not trying to put pressure on you or anything. But he's different with you than I've seen him with anyone else. It's a good kind of change. People have always wanted to be near us—me and Leo—because of what we have and who are parents are, but Leo has never been good at letting people get close."

I snort at that. Can't help it. "You're one to talk."

"Sure." He chuckles softly—almost like Leo. "It runs in the family. But we're not talking about me right now. And there's a way in which I think Leo decided a long time ago that he's never going to get what he wants in love. And he resolved to be okay with it, so he's never given love a chance."

My heart is racing as I listen.

Elias goes on, "He's dated plenty, but he's never taken it seriously. So this is new for him." He shakes his head slowly. "I hope he doesn't freak out and jump ship."

"Thanks a lot."

"He might do it, Lily. Seriously. He's never taken that step before. But it won't be because he doesn't want you. It will be because he's trained himself to believe it's never going to happen for him, so he can't believe it's real."

"Why are you telling me this?" I ask in a trembling voice.

"I don't know. I don't mean to scare you. Maybe it's totally inappropriate. But I think you care about Leo a lot, and so do I. So don't let him push you away."

"I… I… won't."

It's all I can say. I can't even process all the thoughts and feelings swirling through my head. My brain is a blur of fear and hope and confusion and need and longing and excitement.

Honestly, I have no idea what's happening here, but I know more than I did this morning.

I know my daydreams about Elias were nothing but vapor.

And I know that Leo is the one I love.

~

WHEN I RETURN TO our room, I'm in a dither. There's no other word for it.

My stomach is full of frantic butterflies, and my hands are cold and damp. I have absolutely no clue about what I'm going to say or do when I see Leo, but it feels like something significant has to happen.

At last.

I don't see him immediately as I step into the room. "Leo?" I call out, but there isn't an answer. I check the living area and the kitchenette and the bedroom and the bathroom. I pull my phone out of my pocket so I can text and ask him where he is, and then I walk out onto the terrace because there's one corner where I can see down onto the resort beach and outdoor café.

A motion from a chair in that corner makes me jump. I actually jump.

Leo is slouched in the chair, wearing sunglasses and reading a newspaper.

"Oh, you scared me!" I walk over to where he's sitting. "Didn't you hear me call for you? I was looking for you."

"Why?" I can't see his eyes behind the sunglasses, but he doesn't appear to be looking at me. His gaze seems to be focused on the newspaper.

"Because I'm back," I say rather stupidly.

"I see that." His voice is desert dry. No emotional resonance of any kind.

My excited jitters start to shift into something different. Something colder. Heavier. The feeling weighs down my stomach so much I actually raise a hand to cover it. "What's the matter?"

"Nothing. Why would something be the matter?"

"I don't know, but you're acting weird."

"I don't see how. I'm just amusing myself while you take your nice long walk with Elias."

I'm frowning now. I pull a chair over so I can sit down near him. "What is that supposed to mean?"

"It means exactly what I said."

"Are you actually pissed?" I'm so surprised I gape at him. I'm really not sure what I expected from this conversation, but nothing could have prepared me for this.

He arches his eyebrows so high I can see the lift behind his glasses.

"You're pissed," I rasp, my throat tight from surprise and rising indignation. "I just took a walk with him."

"I know what you did. I hope you had a very good time."

"No, you don't. You're being all mean and sarcastic, and you haven't been like this for… for a long time." I'm really upset. Probably more upset than the circumstances warranted since Leo hasn't done anything except make a few sardonic comments. But I just came to some important realizations, and now he's acting like this. "You're the one who told me to do it!"

This comment finally gets a real reaction out of him. He lowers the newspaper and curls his lip. "I did nothing of the kind."

"Yes, you did! This morning. You said I needed to figure out my feelings for Elias, so that was what I was trying to do. You have absolutely no right to act like I did something wrong."

"Not once did I imply you did anything wrong."

"But I know you, remember. You're being all cold and nasty. That means something's wrong. It's not the real you."

"And you think you know the real me now, after a week or two of fucking?"

I rear back like I've been struck. "I don't deserve this, Leo, and I'm not going to take it."

Something happens on his face, but his damned sunglasses are masking it too much for me to really read. But he makes an odd noise in his throat and pushes himself to his feet. "You're right. I'm sorry. You don't deserve it."

Then the asshole walks away from me.

It takes me a minute before I can pull myself together enough to follow him, and then it's too late. He's gone into the bathroom. I hear the shower turn on. I can't imagine he really needs a shower right now since he hasn't done anything but eat breakfast and read the newspaper, but it's probably just a way to get some private time to pull himself together.

That's fine. I can pull myself together too.

And maybe he'll be more himself when he comes out.

I have no idea what to do, so I lie down on the bed on top of the crisp white coverlet that's been newly made up by housekeeping sometime this morning.

Closing my eyes, I breathe slowly and try to make my mind work.

He's jealous. Maybe that's it. It's the most likely explanation for his behavior just now. I'd be jealous as hell if he went off with another woman on his own after spending the past two weeks with me. It's a perfectly natural feeling. Sure, he's not handling it well, but Leo is always going to hide from his feelings.

I'm not all that different myself.

My problem is I don't know if he's jealous because he wants me in his bed or if he's jealous because he wants more than that. It could be either one. He's never said a word about wanting more from me. It *feels* like he wants more, but I've been dead wrong about interpreting feelings before—mine and other people's.

I've been wrong so many times.

The best thing to do is discuss things in a calm, sensible manner and try to get some of the answers I need. I'm an adult. So is he.

Surely we should be able to do that.

My mind is whirling with all the mature, reasonable things I plan to say to him when he finally gets his ass out of the shower. But when I hear the water turn off and him moving around behind the door, I start to panic.

My chest tightens. My throat closes up. My fingers and toes get ice cold.

This conversation could change everything, and not once in my life has a conversation like this gone the way I wanted it to. More often or not, I ended up with a broken heart.

The bathroom door opens, and Leo comes out wearing nothing but a white towel around his waist. He's big and fit and masculine and far too good-looking.

And human. So human it makes me gulp.

He slants me a look, raising his eyebrows in that way he has.

All my mature resolutions fly out the window. "Fuck you, Leo Magnusson," I burst out, sitting up and then hefting myself to my feet.

He blinks. "What?"

The fact that he looks so surprised makes me even more angry. "What, what? You think I won't get mad about this? What exactly do you want from me? Do you want me to figure out how I feel about Elias, or do you want me to never be alone with him again? Because you can't have both."

"Why not?" He looks angry now too but in a cool, tense way. Not a fiery way like me.

"Why not?" I repeat the words because I don't understand them.

"Yes. Why not? I want both those things."

"Well, you can't have them! Can't you see how irrational it is?"

He's moved closer to me, but it seems unconscious on his part, rather than an intentional advance. "Is it any more irrational than being in love with my brother while you're fucking me as some sort of substitute?" The words lash out of him like a whip.

I stumble backward as if hit with a physical blow. "W-what? What the hell, Leo? That's not what I'm doing at all."

"Isn't it?"

"No! I told you from the beginning, and it's never changed. I've been fucking you all this time."

"Have you?" His voice is rough with some sort of intensity. He takes my face in both his hands and scans my expression urgently.

"Yes, you big asshole! You're the one I want!" I'm almost spitting the words out at him. They're not remotely sexy or romantic or appealing in any way.

But they have a profound effect on Leo. He pulls me closer to him. Devours my mouth with a hard, urgent kiss.

I'm not entirely sure of the specific moves that get us there because my mind is a wild blur of need and passion and confusion. But the next thing I know Leo is pushing me down onto the bed and climbing on top of me, pulling off his towel before he kisses me again.

His hands are all over my body. He tears off my top and floral cotton skirt in a clumsy rush. My tank top has a built-in bra, so my breasts jiggle free as he pulls it off. He makes a choking sound and takes one in his mouth, using his lips and tongue and teeth until I let out a sob and arch up off the bed.

I'm clawing at his back and shoulders with my fingernails, trying to get him closer, feel even more of him. When he adjusts to kiss my mouth again, I spread my thighs and drag scratches up the tight flesh of his ass.

He's already hard. His erection is folded up between our bodies, and I try to grind myself against it. I'm more than ready for him, so I shamelessly squeeze my hands between our bodies and try to align him at my entrance. "Leo, please," I mumble against his mouth.

He grunts and raises himself up on one arm, using the other hand to move his shaft into position. Then he's pushing into me, and I'm groaning from the delicious pressure of it. He pushes my knees back toward my shoulders as he eases in so he's deep and I'm folded up beneath him.

He takes me like that, and the buildup of emotions over so long and the intensity of the sensations combine until they overwhelm me. I come and then come again as he thrusts into me, or maybe I just never stop.

We're grunting and rocking wildly and shaking the bed, and it feels like it goes on a long time. So long tears stream down my face, but they're not from discomfort or upset. It's just all so, so much.

As he's nearing the end of his control, Leo grits out, "Lily. Lily. Say my name."

"Leo." The word rasps from my throat.

"Again." He's accelerated his rhythm. His face is tense and damp with perspiration, and his eyes are like nothing I've ever seen before.

"Leo!"

"Again."

I keep repeating his name until I'm sobbing it out with another orgasm. He comes too as my inner muscles contract around him, and he bellows out a wordless sound of completion as he jerks and shakes through his climax.

He collapses on top of me without warning, and I huff as I adjust to his weight. He finds the energy to help me straighten my legs, and then I wrap him with my arms. He's panting against my neck.

"Leo," I say one more time. "It's you I want. *You*."

He grunts.

"Do you believe me?"

He grunts again but doesn't respond with words.

My body is exhausted, still spasming with little aftershocks and a little bit sore. But it feels amazing. The whirl of confusion in my heart and mind have finally subsided.

I would have been perfectly content, holding him close, but I'm aware of a little jittery of worry beneath it.

Because he didn't really answer my question.

Seven

FOR THE REST OF THE DAY and the following morning, Leo isn't terse and sarcastic. In fact, he's meticulously polite. He's also strangely quiet and not at all like himself.

It was very unnerving.

I've known Leo for ages. Nearly all my life. I thought I knew all the various sides to him, but I've never seen him like this before. In someone else, I'd say he was kind and thoughtful and considerate, but I've learned to realize that Leo has always been kind and thoughtful, even in his most sardonic self. This feels more like he's putting on a mask, and I don't like it at all.

Determined to be patient and give him some time, I don't comment on the new attitude. Even when I feel like swatting the gracious smile off his face, I manage to restrain the impulse and just smile back.

The rest of the family doesn't comment on the change or even appear to notice. We have a long, companionable dinner that I would have enjoyed immensely if I hadn't been stewing over what's going on with Leo.

I took a huge step. I told him it was him I wanted and not Elias. It hadn't been easy to admit, especially since he's never admitted to wanting me for anything but sex. I would have thought that would make things better, bring us closer. But it doesn't appear to do so.

We hang out late with his family, and we're both tired when we get back to the room, so we go to sleep side by side in the big bed and don't touch each other at all.

The next morning, I'm hopeful, but Leo hasn't gone back to his regular self. We're flying out to the final stage of our vacation this afternoon, so it's the last morning we have in the Caribbean. I ask Leo if he wants to walk on the beach, and he even goes with me, but he's quiet most of the time except for replying politely to any stray comment I make.

It just makes me worry more.

We have breakfast with his family as usual, and his behavior is evidently significant enough for the others to notice as well. His mother asks him three times if he's feeling all right, and he's not impatient as he responds, even for the third time. His dad wonders aloud why he's not talking much this morning or reading the newspaper, and Elias keeps shooting him questioning looks.

It makes me feel a little better. That his family has noticed something is wrong too. It's not just me making things up in my anxiety-fueled imagination.

Leo blandly ignores all the looks and questions and never alters that weird, quiet smile. We've finished eating when his mother mentions wishing she'd brought her sunglasses out with her since the sun is so bright, and he gets up immediately to go get them for her.

All of us watch as he walks back inside the building.

"What is with the boy today?" Mrs. Magnusson asks.

I shake my head, my eyes burning as I try to control a swell of confusion and grief.

"I don't know," Mr. Magnusson mutters over the last of his coffee, "but much more of this niceness from him, and I'm going to blow my top."

I almost laugh at that, and it comes out as a soft little sob.

Mrs. Magnusson reaches over to pat my arm. "Oh no, are you upset too? Did you two break up or something?"

"I…" I have to take a ragged breath before I get the words out. "I don't know."

"Well, I'm sure you'll work it out. Just give him some time. He doesn't have much experience with serious relationships, poor boy."

I can feel Elias's eyes on me, and when I turn my head, he catches my gaze. He doesn't say anything, but I know what he's thinking.

It's like he was saying yesterday on our walk. He was afraid Leo would run away, that he couldn't believe it was real.

And that seems to be what's happening now.

I work my face until I've caught my breath and push back the tears. "It will be fine." Just an empty thing people say, even when there's absolutely no reason to believe it's true.

"I'm sure it will." Mrs. Magnusson is still patting my forearm. "You'll work it out. He loves you so much. He has for ages."

The words make me stiffen. I check her face, but she appears completely unconscious of any significance to what she said.

It's like she thinks it's common knowledge when it's nothing of the kind.

I'm flushed and emotional and hugging my arms over my belly when Leo comes back with his mom's sunglasses. He sits back down next to me, his eyes slanting over to my face.

For the first time, I see something different in his expression. "What's the matter?"

I shake my head again. It's all I'm able to do.

"What's going on?" he asks in a more demanding tone than I've heard from him since we made love yesterday. "Has someone upset you?" He looks around at his family, as if they might be responsible.

His question is ridiculously ironic. He's the only one who has upset me. I make a face at him and say, "I'm fine. Stop being obnoxious."

Maybe I hope that my remark might kindle our previous banter. The kind of silly argument that feels safe and familiar from him. For a moment, he looks like he's going to snap back a reply, but he pulls it back before it's ever spoken. "You're right," he murmurs. "Sorry about that."

He couldn't have said anything worse.

~

WE RETURN TO THE ROOM with about an hour before we need to leave for the airport. Feeling heavy and depressed, I start to pack up my stuff. I've spread out more here than I did in Prague, so I've got clothes and jewelry and hair supplies all over.

Leo is already mostly ready to go, so he brushes his teeth and packs up the last of his things. Then sits at the desk chair and starts reading something on his phone.

I try to think of something to say that might fix things, but nothing is remotely adequate. I've gotten my stuff packed and am halfway through zipping up my suitcase when all of it is suddenly too much.

I sit down on the edge of the bed and bury my face in my hands.

"Lily?" He's clearly not so absorbed in his phone that he doesn't notice me.

I lower my hands and look over at him. I'm not crying, but my face twists with emotion anyway.

"What's the matter?"

And that just makes me mad. "How can you even ask me that?"

"I'm trying to be good."

"Good? You think this is good?" I wave my hand in a vague gesture that's supposed to encapsulate how he's been acting. "This isn't you. It isn't anything like you. Even if you don't want me, you don't have to act like a stranger."

He stares across the room at me for a little too long. "You know I want you."

"Do you? Because it sure doesn't feel like that. It feels like you're putting up walls even after I told you yesterday that I... I..." I have to clear my throat and take a deep breath. "That I want you and not Elias."

"I know you said that."

"But you don't believe me?"

He opens his mouth just slightly, but no word comes out.

"I'm telling you the truth, Leo. These have been the best two weeks of my entire life. Why don't you believe me?"

Again, it's a long time before he's able to answer. Something is working just slightly on his face, but he has it under complete control. "You've been in love with Elias your entire life."

I make a sputtering noise but try to pull back the automatic defensiveness. "I thought I was. I did. And maybe in some way... But it wasn't ever real. He just somehow became the embodiment of my... my need for love. I channeled it all into him, and after a while I became so used to it that I never even questioned it. But I don't love him, Leo. Not for real."

His gaze is deep and intense and entrapping. He doesn't say anything.

I summon every particle of courage I possess to say, "Leo, please. I… I have feelings for you that are… different. That are real. Can you tell me honestly you don't have feelings for me too?"

"You know I do," he murmurs roughly. "I have for a long time."

I hadn't really known that before, but his words aren't the surprise they should have been. Maybe in the back of mind, I did recognize the truth before. "So then what's the problem here?"

He just looks at me again without speaking.

"Maybe your feelings for me are more like mine for Elias. They're just a made-up fantasy. They're not based on anything real."

He straightens up, his shoulders and back tensing with what looks like indignation. "You know perfectly well that's not the case."

"Then I don't understand why you refuse to try this with me. I think we have something… something good here. I think it's worth… pursuing. I want to give it a try. With you. Don't you want that too?"

He licks his lips slowly. His hands clench and then release on the arms of his chair. "Part of me does want that, but I don't think it's ever going to work."

"Why not?" My voice cracks on the second word.

"Because I'm not sure how a relationship can survive when I'm always wondering if you'd rather be touching my brother."

It hurts so much I gasp.

"I'm sorry," he adds, rubbing his jaw and making a scratchy noise from his stubble. "I really am. But I can't stick the landings, remember. I'm not a closer. I start things I never finish. It is what it is."

"Okay," I manage to say. I get up quickly and hurry to the bathroom.

I don't need to go. But I need to cry, and I don't want to do it in front of Leo.

~

THE THIRD STEP OF OUR journey is Asheville, North Carolina, where Mrs. Magnusson has booked us into a fancy ski resort. I've never skied before since my parents didn't find it a culturally relevant pastime. Under normal circumstances, I would have enjoyed the chance to learn since it always looked like it might be fun.

But the last thing I want to do is try a new activity and make a fool of myself when things are as awkward as they are between Leo and me.

He is acting a little better after our conversation. More like the person he was a couple of years ago—dry and clever and mostly cool without any softness or vulnerability. It's not his whole self. It's not the person I want him to be. But it's better than that polite stranger.

Our room is gorgeous, of course. Simple and spacious with a big four-poster bed and a stone fireplace on one wall. As we walk in, I go over to the window to look out on the snowy mountain scenery.

On a different day, I'd be thrilled. Now it just makes me a little sad that I can't share it with the man I know Leo to be.

"I can get us a room with two beds," Leo says after the bellman leaves. He's standing over his suitcase, which he hefted onto the upholstered bench at the foot of the bed. "If you'd be more comfortable that way."

"It's fine," I tell him. "We did okay before we got together. I'm sure we'll do okay now."

"All right." He looks at me steadily, but I can't read any particular emotion his gaze. "I'm really—"

"Don't you dare say you're sorry again," I say. "You made your decision, and I can live with it. I'm a big girl. And I'm used to not getting what I want."

This has an effect. Something flickers across his face. But he brushes it off almost immediately with a brief shake of his head. "Same here."

If I think about that too much, it will make me mad, so instead, I heft my suitcase onto the dresser and unzip it. "I think I'm going to take a shower. I feel kind of icky."

"All right. There isn't time for skiing today anyway, so I think all my mom is planning is dinner."

"That sounds good."

I get my shower stuff and head into the bathroom. There's a huge walk-in shower, and the water pressure is wonderful. I take a long shower and even wash my hair since it still feels salty from the beach.

When I get out and dry off, I realize I didn't plan well. I didn't bring in my hairbrush, and I don't have anything to change into except the clothes I was wearing, and I don't want to put them back on. So I put on one of the big, fluffy bathrobes hanging behind the door and go out into the main room to get my brush.

Leo is lying fully dressed on the bed, staring up at the ceiling. He did at least take his shoes off.

I want to say something, but everything that comes to mind feels foolish or inadequate. So I bring my hairbrush into the bathroom, leaving the door open to let the steam escape.

I brush my hair and then blow it dry. Since it's long and thick, it takes a long time, but I don't care. At least it gives me something to do.

When I go back to get a soft knit lounge set to change into (since it's more than an hour until dinner and I need something comfortable to wear), I feel Leo's gaze on me.

I immediately recognize the look in his eyes, on his face. "I'm not having sex with you."

"Did I ask you to?"

"No, but you have your sex look on."

"Not much help for that with you going around half-dressed. And all that hair…"

The shiver of pleasure surprises me. "I didn't do it on purpose. It never occurred to me that blow-drying my hair might turn you on."

"It does. Everything about you turns me on." The words aren't a come-on or a sexual advance. They sound like a simple statement of fact.

I take a shaky breath, trying to figure out how best to handle this. "Obviously I'm attracted to you too, but I don't want us to fall into bed again. Not if it... it's not going to go anywhere."

"I understand."

"Sex isn't enough for me. It's good. Really good. Obviously. But it's not... it's not really what I want."

"I know that, Lily. I wasn't going to make a move on you. I mean it."

I nod, my cheeks flushing despite my determination to handle this situation in a smart, reasonable way. "Okay."

Not sure what else to say, I step back into the bathroom. This time I close the door.

THE NEXT FEW DAYS ARE less painful than I would have expected. Leo and I fall into a workable routine of casual talk and careful consideration of each other's boundaries. It's not great—not at all—but it's better than being in a painful fight.

I have no doubt that, as soon as this vacation is over, I might fall into a bleak pit of despair over losing what I almost had, but it hasn't really hit home yet that I've lost him because he's always around. Always looking at me with that intense scrutiny that seems to see into my soul.

It doesn't seem like he's going to change his mind about us, but the way he looks at me makes it impossible to completely give up hope.

I learn to ski—not well but also not too embarrassing. And we have a lot of good meals and cozy evenings by the fire as a family. On Wednesday night, Mrs. Magnusson announces that there's a surprise planned and we're leaving to fly somewhere else the following day.

Evidently this is a brand-new experience. Elias says she's never done it before. Elias, Mr. Magnusson, and I have a long conversation, trying to guess where we're going, but no one has any idea. Leo sits in an armchair, listening to our discussion. He doesn't participate, but at least he hasn't gone off on his own.

Later that night, I take my vibrator into the bathroom so I can have an orgasm before bed, like I've been doing every evening since Leo and I stopped having sex. I think about him as I come. I simply can't help it.

I'm tired and discouraged and heavy as I climb into bed. Leo must be skipping his nightly shower because he's already under the covers. I turn out the bedside light, and we're alone together in the dark.

I want to say something. Anything. Even something completely wrong or inappropriate.

I just want to talk to him again.

"Do you do that every night?" Leo asks into the darkness before I blurt out whatever nonsense comes to mind.

"What?"

He clears his throat, and I suddenly wonder if he's done the same thing I was mulling over—burst out with anything since it's better than saying nothing. "I asked if you do that every night."

He doesn't clarify, but I suddenly know exactly what he's referring to. I gasp and raise my head, trying to peer at him as my eyes slowly adjust. "You know?"

"Yeah." He sounds almost self-conscious about the admission.

"You've known all this time and never mentioned it?"

"I didn't know for sure at first. I thought I was just imagining the sound, and it felt too sleazy to move closer to the door so I could hear better. But you'd always come out so much more relaxed, so I figured it out eventually."

"Oh." I'm kind of embarrassed but not as much as I would have expected.

"So do you always do it?"

"Yes. I can't seem to sleep without coming. The only time I don't is when I have good sex before bed. I don't know why. I just got into the habit. It's probably because of my controlling nature—as you like to point out. It's the only way I can let go enough to sleep."

"Okay."

"Do you think I'm strange?"

He makes a snorting sound. "Are you serious? I've had to get myself off several times a day just from being around you. I told you before that's why I take so many showers."

I stare at him, although I still can't see his face very clearly. "Oh. That's right." I swallow hard. "Good."

"Good?"

"Yes. Good." I pause and finally add, "I didn't want to be the only one."

~

I GO TO SLEEP a few minutes later since I'm tired from the emotional stress and the physical exercise. But I wake up sometime in the middle of the night. I know it's very late. It's pitch-black in the room. The covers have slipped down my body, so I'm chilly.

The most natural thing in the world is for me to seek the warmest thing in the bed, which happens to be Leo's body. I roll over toward him, trying to cuddle up against his heat.

He's been asleep too, and he makes the sound in his throat that he often does when he wakes up. He mumbles something incomprehensible and wraps his arms around me.

I whimper in pleasure as I press myself against him. He feels big and strong and safe and familiar. Exactly where I want to be.

He holds me for a while, both of us relaxed and breathing slowly. Then his hands start moving, stroking over my hair and my back. It feels so good I moan long and low.

The sound must trigger something in Leo. He mumbles something else—once again without real words—and rolls us over so I'm on my back and he's on top of me. He ducks his head and gives me clumsy kisses on my neck.

I could stop him if I wanted. Maybe I should. But I don't want to. This is what I want, and on the edge of sleep like this, I can't stop myself from taking it.

My hands move up and down over his body too, feeling the rippling planes of his back, the thick muscles on the back of his thigh, the firm, tight arc of his ass. He's wearing nothing but a pair of boxer briefs, and he might as well be naked. I can feel him so completely. Every inch of him.

He's growing hard against my middle. He's nuzzling my face and the crook of my neck. He slides his hands under me so he can cup and squeeze my bottom. "Lily," he murmurs thickly. "Lily."

It's exactly what I want to hear. I make a whimper of pleasure and arch up into his weight.

We both fumble around until my gown is pushed up and his erection is pulled out of his underwear. Then he's bending up my knees, and I'm spreading my thighs to make room for him. He's pushing inside me before I know it, and I make a soft cry at how good it feels. How right it is.

"Leo," I gasp as he completes his first full thrust. I've got my fingers clenched in his hair. My legs are bent up around his sides.

"Yes." The word is mostly a grunt as he starts to rock his hips. "Yes, baby."

"Leo." I say it again since he wants to hear it. I know he does.

His motion accelerates. I'm bucking up against his fast thrusts. It's working exactly right for me, and an orgasm is already rising. "Yes," he hisses, jerking his head to the side.

"Leo. Leo, please." I'm clawing at the back of his shoulders as my body tightens in preparation.

"Baby," he rasps, his hips moving vigorously as he gives me what I need.

I cry out loudly as I come, no inhibitions or self-consciousness. I shake helplessly through the spasms of pleasure and dig my fingers into the flesh of his ass.

He jerks and gasps and thrusts a few last times before he's coming too, groaning loudly as he reaches climax. He comes inside me. I feel the spurts of his ejaculation. He drops his head and presses a few more clumsy kisses against the side of my throat as he starts to soften.

I hold him tightly until he starts to shift. Then I clear my throat and straighten my legs. I'm wet and messy between my legs.

We just had sex when neither of us intended it.

"Oh my God," I whisper.

He pushes himself up with obvious effort. He stares down at my face. "Are you okay?"

"Yeah. Yeah. It's just... I'm not sure what just happened."

"I'm sorry." He rolls off me and collapses on his side of the bed. "I shouldn't have... I should have made sure you were fully awake."

"I was awake, but I'm not sure you were. Did you even... did you want to do that?"

"Of course I did." He sounds different now. He's peering at me in the dark. "So you... you knew what you were doing?"

"Yes. I could have stopped you if I wanted. I didn't want to stop. I wanted it, Leo."

"Okay. But we didn't use protection."

"I know. I'm on birth control. We'll probably be fine."

"Okay. Good."

"But..."

"But what?"

"I'm not sure it was smart. Not if nothing has changed." I pause that anxious swell of hope rising into my chest. "Has anything changed?"

"I..." He lets out a long breath. "I don't know. I don't seem to know anything."

"Neither do I." Ridiculously, I feel better than I have since Saturday. I roll over to face him and reach out to cup his cheek. "I guess it's a very confusing situation.

We don't have to have it all figured out right away. We'll just do the best we can. Okay?"

He leans his head against my hand. It's the smallest of gestures, but it fills my heart anyway. He murmurs, "Okay."

Eight

THE FOLLOWING MORNING we fly out early, and I still have no idea where we're going.

I don't mind an unexpected fourth stage of our journey. The change might actually help. Give us something else to think about and talk about. Take some of the pressure off whatever is going on with Leo and me.

Leo is quiet this morning. He hasn't said a word about what happened between us last night, and I'm too uptight and nervous to ask about it.

By nature, I'm the kind of person who likes closure. Decisions made. But I'm terrified in this case that the final decision I hear from Leo will be something that breaks my heart. If that's the case, I'd rather never hear it at all.

So I try to act friendly and natural with the rest of the family, and I must fake it well enough that even Mrs. Magnusson doesn't question me, although she does shoot a few concerned looks toward her uncharacteristically silent son.

We've been in the air for about three hours when I get up to use the restroom, and I stop by the bar to get a glass of ginger ale before I return to my seat. I take my first sip, standing next to the counter. Despite my best efforts, my eyes drift over toward Leo. He's got his seat reclined and his eyes closed. He's acting like he's asleep, and maybe he actually is. I would find it impossible to nap in these circumstances, but people are different.

It bugs me. A lot. The possibility that he might be able to sleep while it feels like my whole world is on the verge of falling apart.

"Everything okay?" The murmured question surprises me, and I give a little jerk, sloshing my ginger ale onto my hand.

I turn and give Elias a small smile. "Fine."

"Don't give up on him."

"Give up?" It's one of those stall questions. Just a way to give myself time to come up with a safe response.

"You know what I mean. He's never done this before."

"I know that. Neither have I, if you want to know the truth. But I'm not sure how it's ever going to work if he doesn't even believe what I say. If he doesn't want to be with me, then he doesn't. There's nothing I can do to change it. You don't expect me to just put everything on hold for a man who doesn't want me."

My voice breaks as I finish the last sentence because the truth is I've been doing this for way too long. Hanging on to a vague fantasy of love and connection and fellowship because I was so afraid to let it go and be left with nothing. And channeling all that neediness into what amounts to a random man—just because he happened to give me a lily once.

I can see now it was a kind gesture but mostly an insignificant one to him. He's never mentioned it or repeated it, and so it never meant what I wanted it to.

I wasn't wrong to crave that intimate human connection. We're made to have it. I just should have looked for it where it might be found instead of waiting for it to appear like magic in the shape of one person.

For several days—just over a week—I felt like I finally had my hands on what I wanted, but now I'm not so sure.

"He does want you, Lily," Elias says, his blue eyes gentler than normal as they rest on my face. "He's been crazy about you since we were teenagers."

"What?" My voice cracks again for a different reason this time.

"You knew that, didn't you? I thought everyone knew that."

"Of course everyone didn't know that. I don't even think it's true. He never said a word to me about it, and he always acted like I was... nothing important to him."

"He doesn't know how to put himself out there. He's lived his life assuming no one but his family will ever really love or understand him. Obviously you can't let him just string you along indefinitely, but I don't think he'll do that. At least give him a few more days."

I let out a little puff of air—almost, almost a dry laugh. "Well, I'm not going anywhere until the end of the vacation. After that…?" I shrug.

Elias nods soberly. "I'll give him a kick in the pants before then if he needs it."

I laugh for real then, my eyes slanting back over to Leo, whose eyes are still resolutely closed. "I always knew you weren't as cool and standoffish as you act. There's a real nice guy there beneath all that coolness."

He blinks. "Do I act that way?"

"Of course you act that way. You and Leo both try to keep people at arm's length as if you're scared to show the good guys you really are. Your dad does the same thing. It's obviously in the genes."

"Oh. Probably so. Well, maybe I'll find someone who can see me for real the way you see Leo."

"I'm sure you will." I give his upper arm a squeeze before I return to my seat with my ginger ale. My gaze lingers on Leo's face, but he just won't open his eyes.

~

WE LAND AT THE CHARLOTTETOWN Airport on Prince Edward Island.

I'm in one of those travel dazes where I hurry from place to place, following signs and trying to keep up, so it's actually a few minutes before I process where we even are.

Prince Edward Island.

The place a couple of weeks ago I told Leo and Elias is the spot in the world I want to visit the most.

It can't be a coincidence.

Can it?

I'm in even more of an emotional blur as I try to wrap my mind around it. The Magnussons are all acting like the destination is no big deal—just a regular part of their vacation. But they've never hit a fourth spot before, and why the hell would they end up here if it wasn't for me?

Did they really do this for me?

I try to bring up the subject as we pile into the fancy chauffeured car that's going to take us to our hotel. "I can't believe we're here," I say, keeping my eyes focused on Mrs. Magnusson. "I've always wanted to come here."

"Oh really?" she asks, a bland innocence in her expression. "How nice. I'm glad it worked out well then. It's a lovely place. It's not the ideal time of year, but every season is gorgeous here."

I can't think of a way to continue the questioning and find out whose idea this is. I keep looking over at Leo for some answers, but he's avoiding my eyes.

So I'm in a bewildered fluster when we get to the charming hotel and are shown up to our rooms. Leo says he needs to discuss some plans with the concierge, so he stays downstairs, and I'm alone when I walk into the room we'll be sharing.

It's lovely. Antique furniture. Nature-themed watercolors on the wall. A big comfortable bed with a clean gray duvet.

On the foot of the bed is a plush darker gray throw blanket that looks as soft as velvet.

On top of the blanket is lying a perfect, graceful calla lily.

I freeze when I see it, barely hearing as the bellman asks if there's anything I need. I do manage to pull myself together enough to tip him, but I'm shaking as he closes the door behind him.

Returning to the bed, I stare down at the lily.

It's exactly like the single lily left for me after my recital when I was eighteen years old.

My chest hurts. Emotion swells up in it so much it feels like it's crushing my lungs. I suck in a raspy breath and sit down on the bench at the foot of the bed.

I try to breathe, but I end up wheezing. I lean forward and squeeze my eyes shut.

My hands tremble. So do my knees. I try to hold it back, but I can't.

I start to cry in tight, aching sobs.

I've hugged my arms to my stomach as I lean over, desperately attempting to hold it all together. But I haven't even made an inroad when the door to the room opens quietly and someone walks in.

Aware of the presence but unable to respond to it, my crying turns into raw, choked sobs.

"Oh my God, Lily," Leo says in a soft, gravelly voice.

In my mind, I straighten up and look at him to tell him I'm fine, but my body doesn't cooperate with my intentions. I cry even louder, burying my messy face in my hands.

Then he's sitting on the bench beside me. Pulling me into his arms. "I'm so sorry, baby. I'm so sorry. I don't know how to do this."

He sounds so upset that everything inside me wants to help him, but my body is completely out of my control. I sob into his shoulder, wrapping my arms around him so tightly it might hurt.

"I don't have any idea what I'm doing," he says, stroking my hair. He smells delicious—warm and clean and natural. Like Leo. "I have absolutely no idea. But I'd never want to upset you like this. I was trying…"

His unfinished sentence intrigues me so much that I manage to pull away from him a few inches. Just enough to look up into his face. "What were you trying?" I ask in a croaky voice.

"I was trying to do better. Show you how I feel without putting any pressure on. Did I mess it up?"

I start sobbing again and throw myself against his chest. He holds me for another minute until I get it together again. Then I mop at my face with my hands—I could really use a few tissues or a big wad of paper towels—and say, "You didn't mess it up."

"Okay. Good." His eyes drop and then lift to meet mine again. "Then why are you crying like this?"

"Was it you?" I rasp.

"What?"

"Was it you? Back then? After my recital. The lily? Was that from you?"

His dark eyebrows draw together. "Yes. Of course it was. Why?"

"Because I didn't know! I didn't know it was you!"

"What?"

"I didn't know!" I wail. "I thought it was your brother."

A fast series of expressions flicker across his face, ending with absolute outrage. "What? Why the fuck would you think it was Elias?"

"Because he was the one I told about the lily. I never told you. You weren't anywhere around. How did you even know about it?"

"I asked him what you two were talking about, and he told me. So I thought..." He shrugs helplessly.

"I didn't know it was from you."

He grows very still. "So... so all this time, you thought Elias gave you that lily?"

"Yes! Why do you think I was in love with him?"

"But... but..."

"I know!" I'm so indignant I give him a little shove with both hands on his chest. "Why didn't you put your damn name on it?"

"I don't know. I was scared. But I figured you knew I had a thing for you, so who else... Why would you think it was Elias? He was never into you."

"I know that now. But I imagined…" The reality of the situation is finally catching up. I dissolve into half tears and half laughter. "Oh my God, Leo. What an absolute mess we've made of everything."

He wraps strong arms around me again. He's rocking me just slightly. "Yes. We definitely have. But I know you're not telling me that you would have fallen for me back then if you knew that lily…"

"Probably not. I wasn't ready. And I already had a crush on Elias. But it became the symbol in my mind that someone finally… finally saw me. Cared about me."

"Well, someone did," he murmurs almost diffidently. "Someone always has. And it wasn't Elias."

"I know that now." I've finally processed the tidal wave of emotion, and I'm limp and exhausted as I lay against his chest. "I love you, Leo. I've been completely clueless most of my life, but I'm not anymore. It was always you who saw me. Knew me. Cared about me. And I should have seen it a long time ago."

He makes a rough sound in the back of his throat and tightens one of his arms. The other is brushing my hair back. "I love you too. I think I always have."

"So you believe me now? That I'm not secretly wishing you're Elias?" I have to draw back to check his face as I wait for an answer.

"Yes." His smile is small and warm and tender. Just slightly shaky. "I believe you. I can't believe it's true, but maybe you really do… want me."

"I do. I want you, Leo. Just you. Only for you."

We hug for a long time, and then he kisses me deeply. It doesn't go any further than that because both of us are exhausted from the overflow of feelings, but it's still exactly right.

The right person. The right time. For us both.

~

THAT EVENING, WHEN LEO and I meet the rest of the family downstairs in the hotel lobby to go to dinner, we're holding hands. Leo doesn't pull his hand away, even in the face of his parents' and brother's stares.

Mrs. Magnusson makes a happy sound and raises one hand to cover a smile with typically dignified discretion. Elias meets my eyes and nods. And Mr. Magnusson snarls and mutters, "About damn time."

That's all that's said. Nothing else is necessary. They all seem to understand that my relationship with Leo is finally settled, and they're all happy about it. They don't need to know why I came on this trip. They never need to know all that. They understood the heart of our situation correctly, and they're happy now that we're happy.

It's more than enough.

We go to a small, upscale restaurant for dinner and sit at a table overlooking the water. The moon is full, and the stars are glittering. It's an absolutely perfect evening.

Not anything like my daydreams of visiting this island—which mostly consisted of vague, silly pictures of running in a field of wildflowers into Elias's arms. But far better. Realer. Richer. Fuller. Leo sits beside me and occasionally reaches over to touch my knee, my hand, or my hair. And everyone is in a warm, laughing mood.

I've never felt like I was part of a family, but I feel that way right now. Like Leo's family is mine as well. Like they want me to be one of them. It's heady. Almost intoxicating. And it makes me feel nearly as good as the warm, deep look in Leo's eyes.

We talk and laugh and make plans for the next two days we'll have here on the island, and it's late when we get back to the hotel. I go to take a shower before bed. I'm halfway through soaping myself up when the shower door opens and Leo steps in with a wave of cool air.

I squeal from surprise and act indignant, but I'm not at all unhappy with his joining me. He helps me soap up, and then I help him and we end up making each other come with our hands.

After we get out and dry off, I'm relaxed and giggling as I brush my teeth and wash my face and put on a pretty pink gown. I brush my hair out and leave it loose. Leo watches me, looking ridiculously appealing in his pajama pants and damp, messy hair.

"You're not going to need your vibrator tonight," he says when I meet his eyes in the bathroom mirror.

"I guess you gave me a pretty good orgasm in the shower," I say, feigning casual disinterest. "But I'm not sure if it's enough to tide me over."

"It's not nearly all you're getting this evening. Just wait."

I can't hold back the shiver of excitement at the throaty texture of his voice.

He's as good as his word. As soon as we get into bed, he moves over me, and he takes his time, kissing and caressing all over my body and bringing me to climax over and over again.

By the time he finally settles himself between my thighs and I wrap my legs around him as he pushes inside me, I'm so spent I'm not sure I can come another time. But he rocks his hips slow and steady, thrusting as he kisses me deeply for a long time.

I never knew I could feel like this. So completely loved. No longer only myself but joined to someone else with more than our bodies. Like our souls are one.

Lofty, romantic thoughts probably prompted by my complete happiness in this moment, but I can't shake them. As his rhythm speeds up and his face starts to tighten, I start to murmur out that I love him. Over and over again. Soon the sensations are rising inside me too, and I can't articulate anything but his name.

But it's enough. The tension on his face shatters as he freezes on the cusp of release. Then his hips jerk hard and fast as he comes, giving me enough stimulation to fall over the edge again myself.

We're both gasping wetly and holding on to each other as we come down and start to relax. He's softening inside me, and eventually he slips out, leaving me very wet between the legs.

I don't mind. In a strange way, it makes it all feel even realer.

He nuzzles the crook of my neck and then finally lifts his head enough to kiss me gently. "I still can't believe this is real."

"I know. I feel the same way. But it is." I've got my fingers tangled in his thick hair, and one actually gets stuck as I try to pull it out.

He winces at the tug and then laughs and pulls me into a hug. "It must be. I can't imagine you'd have pulled my hair like that if this wasn't real."

I know it's supposed to be a supremely romantic moment, but I can't help but laugh too.

~

SIX MONTHS LATER, we're at another fancy party at his parents' place.

I've been talking to Ruth Wilson about her work as an interior designer, and she's been showing me pictures on her phone of her finished jobs. I like her a lot. She's about my age with a sunny but no-nonsense personality that appeals to me. So my interest in her work is real, and so are the oohs and aahs I make over her pictures.

She appears to really appreciate the interest. She's been married to Carter Wilson for almost two years now, but she clearly doesn't feel like an insider yet in Green Valley circles.

I can't blame her. Even having grown up here and paired romantically with one of the Magnusson twins, I still sometimes feel like I lurk on the periphery in larger social gatherings.

We have a really good conversation until Carter's mother calls Ruth over to weigh in on a debate about the best essential oils for calming anxiety. I take that opportunity to retreat from the party for a few minutes, heading into the library to sneak a drink of the good stuff in Mr. Magnusson's bar.

I'm so set on my mission that I don't see that the room is already occupied. Not until a dry voice says from behind me, "That bad, huh?"

I whirl around to find Leo in his favorite chair and reading a newspaper. Predictably. "You scared me. What are you doing skulking in corners?"

"I'm not in a corner. My chair is in the middle of the room. You're the one too oblivious to see me there."

It's entirely true, but I still stick my tongue out at him as I pour myself a small shot of Scotch. "Well, you know me. Always caught up in my own head and oblivious to what's going on around me."

"Very true." He waits until I'm close enough, and then he grabs my hand and pulls me toward him, guiding me into his lap. "Are you upset about something?"

"No. I just needed a little break. What about you? I thought you were outside admiring the work Lincoln's done on that car."

"I was. But then *I* needed a break, so I came in here." One of his hands is cupping my bottom, and I can't help but enjoy how casually entitled it feels.

"That's okay then, but don't stay too long or your mom will get hurt feelings. She's throwing this party for you, after all."

"She's throwing this party because she wants to throw another party. I'm just an excuse."

"Maybe that's true to a certain extent, but she's really proud of you. You defended your dissertation, and your whole committee raved about your work. She's proud of you. Everyone is proud of you." I lean over and give him a quick kiss. "And I'm proud of you too, of course."

He chuckles softly, but I can feel it shaking through his body. "I just did it to prove you wrong about my not being a closer. I can close a few things—if they're important enough."

"I know you can. You closed your dissertation, and all that's left is some paperwork hoops for you to graduate with your PhD in December. And you've also closed a few other things."

"Like what?" He reaches over and gives my lower lip a little tug with his mouth.

"Like me," I admit with a smile. "You closed with me. And I've got to say you really stuck the landing on that one too."

He's still shaking with dry amusement as he takes my head in both his hands to kiss me more deeply. "Good. I'm not about to let you go now that I finally have you."

"I'm glad to hear it, because I'm not going to let you go either."

We start kissing again and are really getting into it when the door to the library opens. Mrs. Magnusson's voice rings out. "Leo? Lily? Are you in here?"

"We are," I say, recovering as quickly as I can as I pull out of the embrace. I'm still on his lap, but there's no help for that at the moment.

She shakes her head, even as she appears to be trying not to laugh. "If you can stop your canoodling for a few minutes, some people here were asking for music. Would you mind playing for us, dear?"

"I'd be happy to," I tell her, scrambling to my feet. "But I hope you haven't been exaggerating my talent."

"I haven't been exaggerating anything," she says with a note of disapproval. "I've only told them that you're the best pianist I've ever heard, which is nothing but the truth."

There's no way not to appreciate her confidence in me. I'm flushed as I start to follow her out of the room.

Leo surprises me by jumping to his feet and falling into step with me.

"What are you doing?" I ask him.

"I'm coming too. You don't think I'm going to miss hearing you play the piano, do you? Of course I'm coming to listen."

So I feel even more melty and have to quickly pull myself together so I don't disappoint anyone with my playing.

I end up doing just fine. And the moment is made even better because Leo's gaze—full of affection, trust, and pride—are on me the entire time.

I guess it's still kind of a surprise to be loved so much, but I'm definitely getting used to it.

Epilogue

SEVERAL MONTHS LATER, I have a long day of music lessons, and I'm hot and tired and irritable as I return home.

We started living together in the spring. Since we were spending every night together, it seemed silly to keep up two separate households, so I moved into his place since it was larger and nicer and had a more expansive view of the lake.

I've never regretted it once. Before, after a day like this, I would have been looking forward to a Friday evening alone to recover from a long, annoying day, but now I'm just looking forward to seeing Leo.

He feels a lot more like home to me than my old place ever did.

Since it's after six, he should be home. Last month, he started on a one-year lecturer contract with a small liberal arts college about a half hour away from Green Valley. He's mostly just teaching their introductory philosophy course, but he's enjoying even that. We're hoping they'll continue to like him there and maybe be able to get the tenure-track position that will open up next year.

Neither one of us wants to move out of Green Valley, but we also want him to have a job he loves in the career he's been working at for so long.

I've parked in the underground parking deck and am debating between the stairs and the elevator when I see Summer Wilson waiting at the elevator, so I go and join her.

She greets me with a warm smile. Like me, she works for Hope House, but she's on the admin side, so I don't see her all the time. She's an heiress of a fortune even larger than the Magnussons. She and her husband, Lincoln, live in the penthouse unit in this building.

Since Summer is quiet by nature, I wait to see if she'll initiate conversation. If she doesn't feel like chatting, there's no need to fake a lot of empty small talk.

"You and Leo need to come over to dinner sometime soon," she says as soon as we step onto the elevator.

I blink at the invitation.

"Sorry," she says with a self-deprecating smile that makes me laugh. "I probably should have prefaced that in some way. Lincoln tells me I'm turning into a hermit lately, so I should think of a few people I like but don't regularly see and do something with them."

"I'd love to do something, and I'm sure Leo would too. He likes you all a lot." Then, out of genuine curiosity, I add, "Why are you turning into a hermit?"

"I don't know. It's not that I want to. I just do if I don't actively try not to. I just go to work and come home and never do anything else. So you want to have dinner sometime?"

I almost laugh again since it's so ironically amusing to think someone as smart and sweet and established in Green Valley as Summer might be worried that people wouldn't want to hang out with her. "I would love to," I tell her. "Just text or call, and we can figure out a day."

Summer looks so pleased with my response that I'm still smiling as I get ready to step off the elevator.

Fortunately, I glance down before I do.

There's a single calla lily on the floor of the hallway in front of the elevator.

"Oh," I say, staring down at it, momentarily disoriented.

"How sweet," Summer says, peering from my face to the flower. "That's got to be from Leo, right? Does he have something romantic planned tonight?"

"Not that I know of." I lean over to pick up the flower before I step off. "I guess I'll see."

Now that I'm looking down the hallway that leads to our front door, I see more lilies, carefully placed every few feet along the path that I'll walk.

I make a little squeaky sound as my heart starts to gallop.

"Oh my," Summer murmurs behind me. "Something romantic is definitely happening tonight. Have fun."

Before I can find my voice, the elevator doors close, leaving me alone.

I start to shake as I lean over to pick up the next lily, and by the time I've collected all twelve that lead to the door, I'm trembling helplessly.

I know what's going to happen tonight.

I know it for sure.

My hands are shaking too much to pull out my keys, but I don't need to. The front door is unlocked and open partway. I push it open the rest of the way and manage to step inside.

The whole entry is filled with lilies. In another moment, I might consider it a ridiculous number of lilies, but right now it's like a dream come true. The room is filled with their fragrance. A couple of tears slip down my cheeks.

I walk through the pathway between the bouquets, still holding the flowers I picked up in the hall, until I turn in to the living room.

Leo is there, surrounded by more lilies.

Kneeling.

And holding an engagement ring in his outstretched hand.

I make the silliest sound. Somewhere between a laugh and a sob.

He quirks his mouth in a very Leo-like look and says, "Not bad for someone who can't seem to stick the landing, huh?"

I make another one of those laugh-sobs. "Not bad? Leo!"

"Wait a second before you jump the gun. I've got something I planned to say."

I raise a hand to my mouth and nod, more tears spilling out.

"A single lily always meant I love you, but I love you so much more now that a single lily wasn't enough. But even this crazy number doesn't come close to the way I feel for you. So I'm hoping you'll want me to love you forever. And be my wife?" His wry voice lifted slightly at the end, making the final words an earnest question.

"Yes! I want to love you forever too!" I drop the flowers I've been holding and stumble toward him just as he rises to his feet, and he's stabilized his stance just in time to brace himself against the way I throw myself into his arms.

So it's touch-and-go for a moment, but we don't both tumble to the floor.

After several rather emotional minutes, Leo's able to slide the ring on my finger.

It fits just right.

He fits me just right.

And I'm laughing more than I'm crying when he kisses me, and I don't ever want him to stop.

Excerpt from Runaway

I'M NOT SURE WHAT WAKES me up. Probably a sound, but not one I can immediately identify. It's dark in the room and smells unfamiliar.

This isn't my one-bedroom apartment in Charlotte—the one I've been living in for five years, ever since I graduated from college. And this isn't a hotel. The Egyptian cotton sheets are too expensive and the mattress too comfortable.

I'm in a guest bedroom in Elias's family home in Green Valley, North Carolina.

And today is my wedding day.

Both of these realizations hit me in the space of two seconds as I become aware of something else.

I went to bed early last night, wanting to be well-rested for day, and I was alone in this room when I fell asleep.

But I'm not alone anymore.

Someone is moving in the dark. I sense more than hear or see him. I barely have enough time to gasp when the mattress shifts and the covers lift, flooding my bare legs with a waft of cool air.

It's then I know who it is.

"Elias, what the hell?" I roll over to face him. I still can't see him clearly, but I recognize the shape and clean, warm scent of him. "You nearly gave me a heart attack. What time is it?"

He laughs soft and husky as he scoots closer. "It's just after six. I did knock, but you didn't answer."

"I didn't answer because I was asleep. What are you even doing in here?"

"I woke up early and wanted to see you." He draws me against the length of his hard, fit body. He's shirtless but wearing pajama pants I can feel against the skin of my thighs.

"It's our wedding day. You aren't supposed to see me until the wedding. Your mom seems very set on that little tradition."

"I know. That's why I came so early, while it's still dark. I can't really see you right now, so we can avoid any inconvenient curses."

"Oh my God, you big cheat." I'm giggling, even as I try to hold onto a stern tone. I can't help but snuggle up against him. "I don't think this is what not being seeing on our wedding day is supposed to mean."

"Close enough."

He kisses me then, soft and deep and deliciously slow.

Elias and I have only known each other for two months, but it feels like a lot longer. Even at the beginning, when the overwhelming attraction between us threatened to consume us, he was always skillful and considerate in bed. He's never really lost control or let primal instinct take over. And he's never failed to make sure he pleases me as much as he can.

I'm not inexperienced. I went out with a lot of guys in college and my early twenties, and I went to bed with quite a few of them. But I still never knew sex could be as good as it's been with Elias.

Even now, I can feel that familiar melting of my body and heart as his tongue delves deep in my mouth and his hands caress over my thin gown. He knows all my most sensitive spots. The pulse at the base of my throat. The peak of my nipples. The soft skin of my inner thighs. He kisses and strokes me with slow, seductive precision until everything else—my grogginess on waking up, my anxiety over the wedding details, everything unknown about my new life and his family—disappear in the wake of the deep sensations.

None of it matters as much as Elias's voice and breath and body and touch.

It's not long before I'm so aroused that I can't lie still. I'm rocking my hips up into the hot weight of him and clutching at his back, shoulders, ass with a fumbling urgency.

"Damn, Jenna," he murmurs thickly, raising his head from the breast he's been suckling. My eyes have adjusted a little, but it's still too dark to see he's face clearly. "You're so hot. So sweet. I love you so much."

154

My heart jumps at the words. At how he really seems to mean them. He's the most self-contained man I've ever known, but in the bedroom he lets down the walls just slightly. I love to sense the real feeling in him as much as I love the way he touches me.

"Love you too," I manage to mumble, my head tossing from one side to the other on the pillow. "Love... you." I arch up dramatically as he takes my nipple in his mouth again and sucks on it hard.

It's true. Entirely true. I've never felt for anyone the way I do for Elias.

But I also get this weird, surreal impression. Like the woman speaking those words and writhing in pleasure under luxury sheets isn't really me.

Jenna Grant. Foster kid. Scholarship girl. Hard-working orphan who's had to fight for every step forward she's taken.

That's always been me. Even after I kept getting promoted in the finance department of a large corporation in Charlotte and made a decent amount of money for the first time in my life. Keep my head down and stay out of trouble. Never take risks or make waves. Hold onto what I've earned for myself. Don't try grasp for more.

I've never really been this woman. The one who can't help but let go whenever Elias Magnusson touches me. The one who's planning a life with him. Who's moving to wealthy, privileged Green Valley to be the wife of the son of a billionaire.

I come hard when he pumps two fingers inside me and then again when he lowers his mouth to my clit. I gasp and whimper and dig my fingernails into the back of his shoulders, so deeply it has to hurt him a little. But I can't help it. I have to hold on or I'll be washed away away entirely, utterly at the mercy of this overwhelming wave of sensation and emotion.

When he shifts position and settles himself between my legs, I've barely managed to catch my breath from the two orgasms. My face is blazing hot. My whole body pulses. The dark shadow of his figure is big and primal. His eyes are a vivid blue, but I can't see them at the moment. I can feel them on me however. Like his hot, possessive gaze might swallow me whole.

"You ready, baby?" His voice is low and gruff. He's holding himself very tensely.

"Yeah. Yeah. Now." I take a loud, shaky breath. "Please, now."

He pulls my thighs farther apart and lines himself up at my entrance. The head of his erection starts to push in, and I arch my neck at the pressure.

Then he's farther in. Easing out and then pushing in all at the way. My inner muscles stretch around the girth of him easily, but I'm still breathless when he's all the way inside me.

He's panting now, propping himself up above me on his forearms. I can occasionally hear a gasped words in his breathing. "Fuck. Yes. Baby. So good."

It is good. Just as good as it's always been with him. It's like our bodies were shaped for each other. I bend my legs and use my heels on the mattress for leverage as I rock my hips very slightly against the penetration.

He makes a hissing sound, and his pelvis gives a small, clumsy jerk.

It thrills me. That tiny motion. I don't even know why.

But I pump my hips even more, until he groans loudly and starts to thrust.

Our motion is an erotic balancing act between my helpless urgency as another climax builds inside me and Elias's skilled control. He angles his thrusts in the way he knows works best for me and bends my knees up toward my shoulders as I try to ride him from below.

It slows us down, but it also deepens my pleasure. I give up trying to hold on and submit to the overwhelming pleasure.

Elias's hips are moving with a steady rhythm, and it just gets better as it intensifies. Gets faster. Harder. The mattress is jiggling and the covers have slipped down our bodies and the soft flesh of my breasts, thighs, and bottom is jiggling. I'm making the most ridiculous sobbing sound as an orgasm grows slow. Unstoppable now.

He leans down to kiss me, muffling the sounds I'm making, which is good because they're getting too loud, and I really don't want anyone else in this house to hear how good he's making me feel.

My back arches up off the bed, and I freeze for a few moments when the climax finally peaks. Then I choke on a cry of release as my body shakes through the spasms.

It goes on for a long time. So long that I still haven't come down when Elias makes as sharp, guttural sound and then jerks helplessly against me. The tension in his body unleashes for those few seconds. I can feel his letting go in his shuddering motion, in his ragged breath, in a sudden softening of his muscles.

I hold him tightly for a moment, both of us caught in the aftershocks. I love how he feels right now. Like he's just as human as me.

It never lasts as long as I want it to. After a few minutes, he lifts his head from the crook of my neck.

I can sense rather than see his smile. "That was a very good way to start the day."

"Yes. It really was." I'm smiling too. I can't help it. My body feels so incredibly good right now—limp, pulsing, boneless, relaxed, so warm. But it still feels like it must be someone else. Some other woman who gets to feel this way. Not the Jenna I've always been.

"And the next time I see you, we'll be getting married. Can't ask for anything better than that." He presses a few light kisses against my mouth. "I love you, Jenna Grant."

"I love you too, Elias Magnusson."

I mean it. I do love him. But it also feels like he's a stranger as he sits up and swings his legs over the side of the bed. He's breathing deeply. Probably catching his breath. Putting on the perfect self-containment with which he always faces the world.

It attracted me from the beginning. That he was so incredibly controlled, but I could still see something real, deep and kind glinting from the blue of his eyes. It felt like a challenge. To find the real man inside. I thought I had but more and more I keep wondering.

It's just been two months. Eight and a half weeks. Before I went to that business conference in Charlotte, I had no idea that Elias even existed in the world.

Then we met. Fell into bed that very night. Could barely get out of bed for the next couple of weeks.

A month after we met, he asked me to marry him, and it didn't feel too soon because he'd consumed my whole world, and I couldn't imagine ever living without him.

I still can't.

A life without him would be barren and empty, so I have no idea why I can't shake this anxiety. This surreal sense of unfamiliarity.

"Are you nervous?" I ask as he slides on his pajama pants in the dark. Elias works out regularly, and his body reflects the commitment. His muscles are firm and well-defined—broad shoulders, straight back, lean hips, strong thighs. If there was more light, I'd be able to see him better, but even the dark silhouette is impressive.

"No. Not at all." He looks down at me. "I can't wait to call you my wife."

"That's good." I smile, and I'm glad he can't see me very well because my smile is a little shaky.

Maybe he senses something. He reaches down and cups my cheek. "Are you nervous?"

"Not really. It's just been a lot of planning and just a month to do it."

"Don't stress about the ceremony. What matters is that we'll be together."

He's saying all the right things. He always has. Like he's the hero of a romantic movie.

But this isn't a movie. It's my life, and my life has never looked like this.

The swell of terror that rises up inside me is enough to make me choke. I hide it with a cough.

"You aren't getting sick, are you?"

"No. No. Just too much crying out in pleasure first thing in the morning. I'll see you later today. At the wedding."

He kisses me, a smile on his lips. "I'll see you then."

about Noelle Adams

Noelle handwrote her first romance novel in a spiral-bound notebook when she was twelve, and she hasn't stopped writing since. She has lived in eight different states and currently resides in Virginia, where she writes full time, reads any book she can get her hands on, and offers tribute to a very spoiled cocker spaniel.

She loves travel, art, history, and ice cream. After spending far too many years of her life in graduate school, she has decided to reorient her priorities and focus on writing contemporary romances. For more information, please check out her website: noelle-adams.com.

Books by Noelle Adams

The Magnussons
> Breakaway
> Runaway

Bad Bridesmaids

The Mistake
The Mission
The Mismatch
The Mishap

Second Chance Flower Shop
The Return
The Rebound
The Reunion
The Remake

Convenient Marriages
A Negotiated Marriage
Married by Contract
A Wedded Arrangement
Wrong Wedding
Christmas Bride

Milford College
Carpool
Office Mate
Single Dad
Secret Santa
Temp

Pemberley House
In Want of a Wife
If I Loved You Less
Loved None But You

Trophy Husbands
    Part-Time Husband
    Practice Husband
    Packaged Husband
    Purchased Husband

The Loft Series
    Living with Her One-Night Stand
    Living with Her Ex-Boyfriend
    Living with Her Fake Fiancé

Holiday Acres
    Stranded on the Beach
    Stranded in the Snow
    Stranded in the Woods
    Stranded for Christmas

One Fairy Tale Wedding Series
    Unguarded
    Untouched
    Unveiled

Tea for Two Series
    Falling for her Brother's Best Friend
    Winning her Brother's Best Friend
    Seducing her Brother's Best Friend

Balm in Gilead Series
    Relinquish
    Surrender

Retreat

Rothman Royals Series
A Princess Next Door
A Princess for a Bride
A Princess in Waiting
Christmas with a Prince

Preston's Mill Series (co-written with Samantha Chase)
Roommating
Speed Dating
Procreating

Eden Manor Series
One Week with her Rival
One Week with her (Ex) Stepbrother
One Week with her Husband
Christmas at Eden Manor

Beaufort Brides Series
Hired Bride
Substitute Bride
Accidental Bride

Heirs of Damon Series
Seducing the Enemy
Playing the Playboy
Engaging the Boss
Stripping the Billionaire

Willow Park Series
>Married for Christmas
>A Baby for Easter
>A Family for Christmas
>Reconciled for Easter
>Home for Christmas

One Night Novellas
>One Night with her Best Friend
>One Night in the Ice Storm
>One Night with her Bodyguard
>One Night with her Boss
>One Night with her Roommate
>One Night with the Best Man

The Protectors Series (co-written with Samantha Chase)
>Protecting his Best Friend's Sister
>Protecting the Enemy
>Protecting the Girl Next Door
>Protecting the Movie Star

Standalones
>Listed
>Bittersweet
>Missing
>Revival
>Holiday Heat
>Salvation
>Excavated
>Overexposed

Made in United States
North Haven, CT
17 March 2022

17257770R00102